Ibrahim Nasrallah was born t[...]
1954, and grew up in a refugee ca[...]
collections of poetry and fourteen [...] [...] [...]
criticism. He is also a painter and photographer.

Gaza Weddings is the third part of his Palestinian tragicomedy, following *Time of White Horses* (Hoopoe, 2016) and *The Lanterns of the King of Galilee* (AUC Press, 2015).

Nancy Roberts is the translator of a number of Arabic novels including Salwa Bakr's *The Man from Bashmour* (AUC Press, 2007), for which she received a commendation in the Saif Ghobash–Banipal Prize for Translation. She is also the translator of Ibrahim Nasrallah's acclaimed *Time of White Horses* and *The Lanterns of the King of Galilee*.

Gaza Weddings

Ibrahim Nasrallah

Translated by
Nancy Roberts

hoopoe
AN IMPRINT OF AUC PRESS

First published in 2017 by
Hoopoe
113 Sharia Kasr el Aini, Cairo, Egypt
420 Fifth Avenue, New York, 10018
www.hoopoefiction.com

Hoopoe is an imprint of the American University in Cairo Press
www.aucpress.com

Published by arrangement with Rocking Chair Books Ltd and RAYA Agency for
Arabic Literature

Exclusive distribution outside Egypt and North America by I.B.Tauris & Co Ltd.,
6 Salem Road, London, W4 2BU

Dar el Kutub No. 26187/16
ISBN 978 977 416 844 4

Dar el Kutub Cataloging-in-Publication Data

Nasrallah, Ibrahim
        Gaza Weddings / Ibrahim Nasrallah.—Cairo: The American University
    in Cairo Press, 2017.
            p.   cm.
            ISBN 978 977 416 844 4
            1.   Arabic Fiction—Translation into English
            2.   Arabic Fiction
            I.   Title
            892.73

1 2 3 4 5   21 20 19 18 17

Designed by Adam el-Sehemy
Printed in the United States of America

It was one of those heavy nights

AND THAT'S PUTTING IT MILDLY.

I thought of writing a journalistic report called "Who could sleep?" but I didn't. It was enough just to scribble my thoughts down night after night to realize what was going down in Gaza.

It was one of those heavy nights.

I don't know when I managed to shut my eyes, although I've begun to wonder whether I actually close them even when I'm asleep.

And who could have stayed asleep anyway?

The knocks on the door would have jarred me awake.

Everything gets all mixed up in this puny head of mine. My mother used to say to people, "Look at that one with the little head, and her sister. One of them alone has more sense in her noggin than the whole lot of you. If God had given me nothing but daughters, I'd be the happiest person in Gaza!"

I liked to hear my mom say that. But it bothered me, too.

It's a bummer to have a little head in a country that's full of big sticks and people who point gun barrels at you all the time.

1

But in the end I decided I was fine with my head, small as it was, and, unlike my twin sister, I took the appropriate precautions.

I did my best to keep my head out of the billy clubs' range, since a single blow would have been enough to smash it to smithereens. At the same time I said to myself, "As long as it's no bigger than this, snipers will be sure to miss it." (Time would tell, though, how wrong I'd been about that.)

These are the sorts of thoughts I used to have during the first intifada. But now I'm not sure whether I still think the same way, or whether I'm just remembering the way I used to think.

The bombing had been going on for so long—with shells, missiles, tanks, helicopters, and even fighter planes—I couldn't tell the different sounds apart any more. A lot of people used to brag that they could tell you exactly what kind of weapon they were hearing. But I wasn't one of them. In fact, I was always amazed at people who could do that. I mean, when all the sleep you get is a tiny snooze that you manage to fall into by a miracle in the wee hours of the morning, how are you going to be able to tell the difference between banging on a door and bombs going off?

"They've started shelling again," said my mom. "Or is that somebody pounding on the door?" (So, then, I wasn't the only one.)

I got up. I knew nobody else would. The only other person in the house was my grandmother, who was holed up as usual in her room because, according to her, the sound of the gunfire didn't reach it so easily.

"Good morning."

"Good morning to you."

"Is your mom home?"

"Yeah, she's here."

"And your dad?"

"My dad? He's in prison, you know that!"

"Oh, I forgot, damn it all."

"On account of the occupation!"

"Of course. What else is there?"

"Come on in."

"Sorry, I can't right now. But I wanted to make one request." After a pause, she went on, "Well, I've always dreamed of having a daughter like you or your sister. And with your help, I can make the dream come true!"

"What do you mean?"

"I mean, your sister will be my daughter!"

"And who said she wasn't your daughter already?"

Ignoring my question, she went on, "My son's grown up now, and your sister's a sweet young lady. And nice-looking, just like you! As you can see, the world's a stinking mess. But still, I was thinking this would be the best time to find him a wife, and I was wondering if you could talk your mom into letting him marry your sister. With your dad being in prison and all, some people might say it isn't proper, that the timing's not right. But what can we do? If we wait till things get better—till the occupation's over and Palestine's free and we get our land back—we'll be waiting forever. Nobody will ever get married and have families!"

I was tongue-tied. I just stood there in the doorway, feeling limp as a rag. Some time later—during which I suppose she must have said a lot—I found myself mindlessly nodding my head. And she must have interpreted my nods the way she wanted to.

She took a couple of steps forward and planted a kiss on my forehead.

"Like I said," she went on, "you're the only one who can help me, and I have a feeling everything's going to be just fine."

Then she turned to leave. I reached out to stop her, taking hold of her long black dress. She looked back at me.

"Come in," I urged. "We can have a cup of tea together, at least, and some breakfast."

"No, no," she protested. "We can have the tea later. And I'm not hungry. I'll go home now and get some things I need, and then I'll go put his mind at rest. You know, the kid's been sweet on her for a long time now. I'd just been waiting for him to get old enough for me to do something about it. I know she's a little older than he is. But now he's sort of caught up with her, if you know what I mean. Have you ever seen anybody so in love? Today's his birthday, and I'll have a little party. Why don't you come over? After all, you and she have the same aura."

4

She stopped talking, lost in thought.

I stood there gazing at her. She seemed worn out, and looked older than usual. All the burdens she'd had to carry would have crushed an oak tree, but she still stood as tall as ever.

"I'll give the boy the good news, and you can tell your sister. What do you say?"

For the second time I found my head nodding without knowing what this meant. And like before, she took my nodding to mean what she wanted it to. Rushing toward me, she gave me another kiss on the forehead. Then she stepped back a bit, looked me over thoughtfully, and said, "You're all I have in this world, bless your heart. I feel better now. Believe me, if I had another son, I'd marry you to him!"

"Seriously, Auntie Amna? I don't need proof of how much you love me!"

Her eyes filled with tears. She turned to go, and I watched her walk away, her headscarf flapping in the breeze.

"Who'd come knocking on our door this time of the morning?" wondered my mother out loud, her eyes still half-closed.

"It was the sound of shelling," I told her.

"I knew it must be. But I thought maybe I'd been dreaming. To hell with them all! They've turned our nights into days! Don't they ever get tired? Are they so deaf they can't hear the bombs they set off?"

After my head was under the comforter, she asked me, "What time is it?"

"Six."

"Six? Get up, then! Haven't you slept long enough?"

I told them it was nearly noon

My husband, my son, and my brother were still asleep. I told them over and over again how late it had gotten, but none of them even budged. "What is this?" I said. "How did you get so lazy all of a sudden? You didn't used to be like this! Now up and at it. It's time to wake up and see the sun, at least, and talk with me a little before I go."

I told them the tea and breakfast were ready, and that we needed to talk, since I'd had some things on my mind for a long time. But they just went on snoozing.

How in God's name had they gotten to be such sleepy-heads? I swear, if I were just a tiny bit meaner, I would have yanked those covers off them and tossed them across the room! But I didn't have the heart to.

You've been a softie since the day you were born, Mustafa! Who could have wished for a more tender-hearted brother? I mean, you stayed with me when everybody else left me behind. Some went to Jordan, some to Syria, and some even made it as far as Sweden.

When my other brothers started getting wanderlust, you told them, "I know every one of you hears himself being called in one direction or another, and that that's the only voice he can hear. Then he'll follow the voice until he disappears into it." Who else would have talked that way, Mustafa? You sounded so wise—like a philosopher or something! And when they made fun of you, saying, "And you, Mr. Mustafa, what direction are you being called in?" you just pointed to the ground.

"Come on!" they said. "The ground isn't a direction. It's a place!"

"Well," you told them, "all directions meet here, on the ground, so whoever's on the ground owns all the directions, too."

God, what you said that day made me so happy! And it wasn't because it meant you'd be staying here in Gaza with me after I got married. No, it just made me happy. It made Randa happy, too, when I told her about it.

She liked it so much, she said, "Can I write that down?"

"Sure," I told her. So she scribbled it in her notebook.

I mean, how many Mustafas do I have? You're the one who insisted that I go to school and get a college education.

Forgive me, Mustafa, but I have to say this: if you're not taken away from here by your concern for your children, you'll be carried off by your hormones—by the urge to chase a dream far away from this misery of ours on the Gaza Strip. But don't get me wrong: I know that even if you were married

8

and had twenty kids to worry about, you'd stay here with me. You said so yourself, though not directly, when you asked, "And Amna, who'll be here for her?"

I know I didn't hear it with my own ears, but I'm sure that's what you must have said. And I'll bet they were glad to hear you talking about some other reason to stay. I heard them whispering, "At least there's somebody who'll stay and take care of our sister."

And you did stay. You told them, "According to a certain Palestinian legend, God creates people out of two kinds of soil: the soil in the place where they were born, and the soil in the place where they'll die. You and I were made from the first kind: this is where we were born, and this is where we'll die. The soil that's calling my other brothers might be in the places where they'll die. But what's calling us is the soil right under our feet. That's how it's been from the very start. And who of us can't hear a call that's that clear?"

You remember the story of Muhammad Musa Abu Jazar? It confirms what you told them. I mean, how else could you explain it? A man goes away for forty years, and while he's gone he fights battle after battle somewhere else. Then he finally comes back to Palestine, and dies defending Rafah—right here in our back backyard!

So now I understand what you were saying to them. I get it now, Mustafa. Like, all of a sudden the light went on. I know now why you pointed to the ground. It's because you could hear it calling, even though you weren't telling me so.

9

It doesn't matter whether I'd heard that legend before or not. What matters is that we feel it, since it's inside us. I can hear it running in your blood.

So why didn't they get it, too? You were always at least ten steps ahead of them. I don't mean to exaggerate, of course. But I remember how, when Jamal came to ask for my hand, he got all flustered over a question that shouldn't have come as any surprise, since it's the question every dad asks somebody who comes wanting to marry a daughter of his. He said, "How do you know the girl?"

Well, the poor guy didn't know what to say! He told me later that when he heard that question, the sky fell in, and it was full of clouds. He used to laugh whenever he told the story again: "Like, all of a sudden I was sopping wet. And it wasn't sweat! If it had been, I would have felt it trickling down under my clothes. As it was, though, it was coming from under my clothes, and from on top of me, too!"

"So," my dad said to him, "you mean to say you're in love with her?"

Then the idiot had the nerve to say, "And is a man supposed to marry a woman he hates?"

"Are you making fun of me?" my dad roared. "In that case, I haven't got any eligible daughters!"

You're the only one who stood by me, Mustafa. You tried to make me feel better. You told me not to worry.

"Don't worry!" I yelled. "What do you mean, don't worry? If we don't get engaged now, then when will it ever happen?

When he gets back from Egypt? He's not going to graduate for another four years, and God knows what might happen between now and then!"

But you just said it again: "Don't worry!"

I thought: since you said it twice, you must know what you're talking about. So I didn't bring it up again.

Then you told me, "Don't lose touch with his family. Go visit them. They like you. Go on acting as though you're one of them—their son's fiancée, his future wife."

"You think that would work?" I asked.

"Of course," you said.

"But Baba would blow his top!"

"Blow his top?" you said. "I don't think so. That would only happen if Jamal were here in Gaza and not away in Egypt. Then again, he might. But only at first."

And things happened just the way you said they would. Just exactly. He ranted and raved. He fumed and he fussed. You told him, "She's visiting his sisters. They're her friends. Jamal's in Egypt, and the only people home are his mom and dad and the girls," but he just shouted, "Regardless—she's not going to see them. She's not going to see them, you hear?"

Even so, I spent more time at their house during those years than I did at home. After a while he stopped asking me where I'd been. He saw how happy it made me to be with them. I don't know why he felt the need to act the tough guy. Maybe it's just because he was a father, and we were up to our ears in worries.

Then one day he called me and said, "Listen, Sweetie, I think you should marry the guy. The best place a girl can be is in a household where her in-laws love her more than they do her husband. I see now how much they care for you!" He paused for a second or two. Then he added, "As for him coming and saying that he's in love, we can't have that! You get me?"

"Yes, sir," I said. Then he burst out laughing. "What? Do you really think I'm serious?"

Then he went on laughing, and he kept laughing until he died. May he rest in peace.

When I think back on that, I laugh so hard that things get out of hand, and I have to cry a little. But now that I'm crying, I don't know if my tears are tears of joy or sadness. You guys have got me all confused.

Anyway, it's nearly noon! How did you get so lazy all of a sudden? You didn't used to be like this. You've way overslept. So up and at it. It's time to see the sun, at least, and talk with me a little before I go.

Mustafa, don't forget—you're the boy's uncle. And you, Saleh, get up and see your birthday sun. Don't let it pass you by! This is the start of your new year, your lucky year. Come on, silly boy! Does anybody in his right mind let his own sun pass him by, the sun that's rising just for him? Look out the window! There's no haze today. No smoke, even. Do you know how long I've been waiting for this day to come?

I counted the days for so long that I'd lost track of time. Then I woke up one morning and, lo and behold, you were all grown up! And now I'll tell you a secret. But don't tell anybody. Don't even tell the ground, since then the wind will find out about it. I've been thinking this over for a long time now, and I've decided that the best thing is to have you and Lamis get married.

You still don't want to get up?

The tea's getting cold while you three lie around like lazy bums. By God, I don't know why I even go to the trouble to make it every day!

As for you, Mustafa, listen: if you don't get up, I'm going to go ask for the girl's hand myself.

. . .

You're not going to? Fine, then! If Saleh wakes up before I get back, don't you dare say anything to him. I want it to be a surprise.

Sometimes days go by

SOMETIMES DAYS GO BY WITHOUT my seeing my brothers Jawad and Salim—in fact, without my seeing anybody at all.

They come by the house quick as lightning, usually in the dark. They kiss our mom's hands and check to make sure we're all right, not realizing that we're the ones checking up on them.

But sometimes it's quite a while before I see them again.

That doesn't mean I spend my days behind some locked door. In fact, I may be the only one who can't stand to stay in one place longer than I've got a mind to.

My mom says to me, "You're always in such a hurry. Why can't you sit still?"

"I don't know," I say, "I just feel as though I'm sitting in a frying pan over a hot fire."

I go out into the street and look around, but I don't see anything.

There are so many of us squeezed into this little strip of land, I can hardly see anybody right.

We're crammed into our houses, into the streets, into the schools, into the marketplaces. In fact, we're so starved for open spaces that if we looked at the sea even for a moment, our eyes might swallow it up.

And we've got more sorrow than we can bear. One time my grandma said, "In order to hold all this pain, we'd need bigger hearts." It took me a long time to figure out what she'd meant by that. When I did, I asked her, "With life being so hard and all, how do you explain the fact that our dreams have never gotten any smaller?"

She turned to look at me. "What do you mean?" she asked.

"Well," I went on, "some years ago you said, 'In order to hold all this pain, we would need bigger hearts.'"

"I said that?" she exclaimed, incredulous.

"Yep. You did. I've even got it written down in my notebook."

"Well, if I said something like that, and if you wrote it down, then it must be true."

"So then," I pressed her, "what about our dreams?"

"Our dreams have never gotten any smaller because they were so small from the start. They were born small and they've stayed that way. And that's why we go on taking care of them all our lives. If dreams were big, they'd be the ones taking care of us."

"Can I write that down?"

"Sure. But don't add anything of your own."

Of course, I didn't get to hear her spout wisdom like this at just any old time. I had to create the right mood for one of her epiphanies. But that wasn't super hard to do. All I had to provide was eight ounces or so of roasted watermelon seeds and a big cup of coffee, which she would follow with a shell-cracking session and a long soliloquy on how much stronger her teeth were than girls these days. It also had to be between nine and ten at night. This was the only time when she'd be willing to say the kinds of things I wanted to hear. And then she'd go to sleep.

"Nothing relaxes me like a cup of coffee!" she used to say to me.

And then, sure enough, she'd be off to the Land of Nod.

Some nights she'd wake to the sound of bombs exploding. She'd come and wake me up, too, and say, "Where did you buy the coffee last time?"

"From Abu Masoud," I'd tell her groggily.

"Well, then, don't buy it from his store again. His coffee's so weak, a single bullet whizzing through the air is enough to wake me up. Next time buy it from al-Maghrebi—theirs is the only kind that'll keep me asleep till seven in the morning."

My sister had tons of girlfriends, but for a long time my only friend was my grandma—at least, until Amna moved in next door. Grandma said, "Thank God for that nice new neighbor lady, since now I don't have to put up with your questions all the time!"

My mom added, "The girl can't sit still for more than five minutes at a time. She's always running around the neighborhood, but she can't make a friendship that lasts more than a couple of days. If she can't find somebody to pick a fight with, she picks one with her shadow!"

"Well, what do you want me to do?" I retorted. "Put on a polite front all the time? When I get to know a girl, I find out that what she needs is a babysitter, not a friend. They're all so dumb and immature!"

"Well, if it isn't the genius of the century talking!" my mother mocked.

"Yeah," my sister chimed in. "She thinks she's Taha Hussein."

"Taha Hussein who?" Grandma wanted to know. "Is he a relative of ours?"

"He's a famous writer, Grandma," replied my sister.

"Oh, like a notary public?"

"No, he wrote books."

"You mean, like the registers people have to sign when they get married?"

"No, like the books we read in school."

"Oh, well, then, why didn't you say so in the first place? You didn't have to embarrass me like that."

"Sorry, Grandma," my sister apologized. She looked daggers at me out of the corner of her eye as if to say, "See? I passed the test, and you failed for the zillionth time."

Amna was like a breeze that blew down our street one day, slowed up a bit, took a liking to the place, and decided to stay.

When she knocked on our door, I was the first person in our house to see her.

She was so beautiful she could have been a movie star, and she looked a lot like the Egyptian actress Athar al-Hakim.

"Are there any houses for rent around here?" she asked.

"For rent, no," I told her, "but there's one for sale."

"For sale? We hadn't thought about buying a house, and I don't think we could afford to."

The way she spoke to me made me feel as though we'd known each other for years. And she talked to me the way she would to a grownup, not to a little girl staring out a half-open door. Emboldened, I opened the door all the way.

"So," she said, standing there uncertainly, "where's the house that's for sale?"

I pointed to the house next to ours. "It's that one," I said.

She took two steps back and looked blankly in the direction I was pointing. Then she crossed the street and gazed at the house as I gazed at her.

She walked back toward me. "It's got a palm tree in front of it!" she exclaimed.

"Yeah," I said. "There's another one, too, but you can't see it from outside the wall."

"Thank you," she said, and left.

Long days passed, but I didn't forget that face. I told Grandma about the lady who'd come asking about houses for rent, and how she looked like Athar al-Hakim.*

"You mean she looks like the doctor?"

"Grandma, al-Hakim is her father's name."

"Whose father?"

"Athar's."

"Oh, so do antiquities have fathers the way people do?"

---

* *Al-hakim* means 'the doctor' in the Levantine dialect in Arabic; *athar* in Arabic means 'antiquities.'

"Grandma, Athar al-Hakim is the name of an Egyptian actress who stars in movies and TV shows."

"Oh, really! So do people have to buy names for their kids in Egypt? Is 'Antiquities' the best he could do? Supposing they did buy names there, he could have afforded one a lot better than that, especially if he's a doctor!"

"Grandma, people don't buy names."

"You think I don't know that? Of course they don't! But that's how the saying goes."

"But honestly, Grandma, her first and last name together, don't you think they're pretty?"

"If you want to know the truth—and don't get mad at me now!—no, I don't. But take my name, for example—Wasfiya—don't you think it's prettier than all the names they're giving girls these days?"

"Of course!"

"Well, there you have it. You said so yourself."

One day I heard a knock on the door. I went out, and there she was, right in front of me. I was over the moon. And when I saw men unloading a truck in front of the house next door, I got so excited that I forgot to invite her in. I just left her standing there and ran back inside screaming happily, "Athar's going to be our neighbor! Athar's going to be our neighbor!"

"Athar who?" my sister asked.

"Athar al-Hakim."

"Are you crazy? What on earth would bring Athar al-Hakim to Gaza?"

Even so, she jumped up and ran to the front door.

A minute or so later she came running back shouting, "It's true! It's true!"

In response to the unexpected squeals of delight, my mother headed for the door, grumbling, "It would be nice to see you two half this energetic when I ask you to do something for me. What's all this silly jumping up and down?"

"Hello," we heard her say.

We stood behind our mom fuming over the fact that she didn't recognize the celebrity who'd graced our doorstep, and was greeting her the way she would have greeted any old neighbor lady. "Hello"—was that all she could think of to say?

By this time I'd forgotten our new neighbor was just some-body who looked like Athar al-Hakim, and not Athar herself, especially now that my sister believed what I'd said. "Boy, what a dummy I am," I thought.

"Hello," Amna replied. "I just thought it would be nice to greet my neighbors before I settle in. Like they say, *al-jar qabl al-dar*." Then she added, "I'm Amna, Umm Saleh." As she spoke, she pointed happily to her rounded belly, which I realized I was noticing for the first time.

"Welcome," murmured my mother. "I'm Umm Jawad. Come on in."

"Another day, hopefully."

"Umm Saleh!" my sister cried suddenly.

"Umm Saleh!" I parroted.

"And pregnant too!" she added.

"And pregnant too!" I parroted some more.

"So, then," my sister mused, "she can't be Athar al-Hakim after all."

"She is too!" I insisted. "She must have given up her acting career to take care of her family."

"But her name's Amna, not Athar."

"Yeah, that's her real name for sure. Don't you know that actresses and actors take stage names? Just wait, and you'll see that I'm right."

When we saw her husband a few weeks later and found out he'd studied in Egypt, that cinched it for me. "See?" I crowed to my sister. "So do you believe me now? They must have met and gotten married there. Then she decided to move here with him."

"Do you really think Athar al-Hakim would be crazy enough to leave her acting profession and come here, of all places? And for what? To get married? Don't you suppose they've got enough eligible bachelors in Egypt?"

"Seriously, now," I argued, "if you were an actress and met somebody that looks like her husband, wouldn't you leave your profession?"

She was quiet for a while. Then finally she said, "Yeah, I would, actually. In fact, I'd leave acting and the whole shebang for a guy like that."

"Aha! So you admit it. She *is* Athar al-Hakim!"

"No, I didn't say that."

When my mom decided to pay Amna a visit and take her a set of coffee cups, we begged her to take us with her.

When she opened the door, I was so excited I was shaking. Even my sister, who'd kept on telling me our new neighbor wasn't Athar al-Hakim, was all pumped up.

"So," she wanted to know, "which of you is Randa, and which is Lamis?"

"I'm Lamis," my sister announced.

"No, I am," I contradicted.

"Here we go again!" groaned my mother.

We sat quietly in the tiny guest room while the two women talked about all sorts of things, but we didn't hear a word they said. We were too engrossed in our new neighbor. When our mother signaled that the visit was over by standing up, the two of us burst out in unison, "Are you Athar al-Hakim?"

As we stood there, clinging to our mother's dress from opposite sides, she looked at us oddly and said, "Athar al-Hakim? Who's that?"

"Don't you even know who she is?" we cried, crestfallen. Then we didn't say another word.

When she saw us standing there frozen like statues, she responded with a giggle that brought us back to life.

"Of course I know who she is! But do I really look that much like her? This is the first time anybody's asked me that question."

She bent down and gave my sister a kiss. Then she circled around my mother, found me in my hiding place, and gave me a kiss, too.

"So," my sister snorted as we got to the door, "are you finally convinced that she's not Athar al-Hakim?"

"Well, yeah, but only because she's prettier than her."

Jamal! Jamal!

"It's gotten to be nine o'clock, Jamal. I went to their house and I saw her sister, Randa."

. . .

"What do you mean whose sister? Lamis's, of course! I talked to her about it, and you can't imagine what a great girl she is. If he liked her even just a little, I'd match him up with her instead. But like they say, the heart wants what it wants. Her mother always calls her 'little head.' Like Lamis, she's still pretty and petite, just the way I remember her from the first time I saw her. I'm the same way with you: to me you'll always be the guy who's going away to Egypt, scared of any city other than Gaza. Now don't get me wrong. It isn't just because I hold onto this image of you, but because you really are still tall and handsome the way you were before. Just look at you: there isn't a gray hair on your head!"

. . .

"But there's something I've never been able to figure out. There are people I first knew when they were even younger than their children are now. Yet I can't seem to imagine a son being older than his father or a daughter being older than her mother no matter how long they live—even when their hair turns gray and starts to fall out, their backs are stooped, and they get cataracts. You know what I mean?"

. . .

"I remember meeting people way back who were older than I was—some just a little older, others a lot older. Then later they died, and now I'm a lot older than they were then. But when I remember them I still think of them as being older than me, the way they were when I knew them before."

. . .

"You're going to get me off the subject by saying things like that, Jamal! I'm going to forget what I was talking about!"

. . .

"Anyway, I saw her."

. . .

"'Who?' you say? Are you still asking me who? I saw Randa! I said, 'Randa, sweetie, I know your daddy's been in prison for the last twenty years. But even so, we've got to go on with our lives.' Well, I might not have said that. But I'm not lying to you, since if I saw her again, that's exactly what I'd tell her, word for word. It's what I should have said. But when I went over there, I was flustered. You know how it is. Whenever the suitor's family go to the girl's house, they take one step forward and one step back. So I was afraid I might say the wrong thing and mess things up! You remember what my dad did to us when he rebuffed you? It was a different situation, of course, since, when a guy asks for the hand of a girl he's in love with and she's in love with him too and her father says no, they both feel terrible. But the issue is more complicated here. Lamis and Saleh are in love, of course. That's no secret, even though Lamis has always kept quiet about it. The problem is that Randa is older than Lamis. Granted, there's only a difference of five minutes between them, but she's still the oldest. So as far as her parents and brothers are concerned, she's the one who should get married first. That's why I wanted to talk to Randa before anybody else, since I didn't want anybody to hurt her feelings by saying something like, 'See? Your little sister got married before you did!' You see what I'm saying?"

. . .

"I want her to feel as though she's the one approving her sister's engagement—that she's the one giving permission. Besides, you have to remember that Randa's my friend. True—I still see her the way I did the first time we met: as this little girl hiding behind her mother and thinking I'm Athar al-Hakim. I've never told you this before, but that really made me happy. I hadn't told you because I didn't want you to think I was conceited."

. . .

"Oh, God, what have I done? Here I am telling you, even though I didn't want to! I swear to God, I didn't mean to tell you that!"

. . .

"Anyway, I know you believe me, honey. So what was I saying . . . ? Oh, I was saying that this is hard for me. I'm only human, after all. But Randa took it hard, I think, because she said to me, 'I thought I was your friend, and that you loved me the most. I thought that when you decided to look for a wife for your son, I'd be your first choice.' You see what a mess I'll have gotten myself into if I can't find a way to explain this to her?"

. . .

"If you want to know the truth, Randa *would* be my first choice. I've got to lower my voice. I wouldn't want Saleh to overhear me. But the boy's been in love with Lamis since . . . no, I won't tell you that. I won't say. . . ."

. . .

"Are you mad now? All right, then, I'll tell you."

. . .

"You say, 'So, he's been sweet on her since the first gust of wind that blew her dress up?' Now where did you hear that? I don't remember telling you! And there's no way the boy would have said so himself. He didn't even tell me, and I'm his mother! But if you're right, then it means the boy grew up while I wasn't looking. In any case, that isn't why he fell in love with her. It started a long time ago, and then developed later on."

. . .

"You know how we hold onto the images we first formed of people. The best example I can think of is the way we look at our own kids. No matter how old they get, we go on seeing them as our babies!"

. . .

"You get me now, right? Of course, we'll marry him off and he'll have kids of his own. We hope so, anyway! And then I'll be a grandma and you'll be a grandpa. But even then we won't really believe he's a father, just the way nobody who's known us for a long time will believe we've become grandparents."

. . .

"When we like somebody, it's usually based on our first impression. Why is that? It really bugs me. I don't think about it night and day, of course, and I don't want to give you a headache by talking about it. But I think we hold on to our first impressions of people because we know deep down that sooner or later they're going to change."

. . .

"Hey, don't laugh at me! I've thought a lot about this, actually, and I've decided that people are like cameras. That's right—cameras. Now there you go laughing at me again! If you don't want to hear the rest, never mind. I won't say another word."

. . .

"So you aren't laughing at me, really—you're just putting up politely with my silliness?"

. . .

"The idea of the camera is strange, I've got to admit. And why should I tell you about it? Should I just blabber on about this and that? When you tell me everything I say is worth saying, are you being honest, or just polite?"

29

. . .

"Well, thank you."

. . .

"So even silly things are worth saying?"

. . .

"What do you mean?"

. . .

"Now we're back where we started. I swear I'm going to get mad. I'll stop talking to you, and you know I'm serious, since I've done it before. One time I stopped speaking to you for days because I thought you'd stopped listening to me. Well, that's a mistake I don't plan to repeat. And in case you're wondering, I'm not saying that to please you. I really mean it."

. . .

"Do you want me to go on? So what were we talking about? Oh, yeah . . . we were talking about people being like cameras. And they really are. For each person we know, we take just one picture. Of course, nobody knows how long a person's 'film' is, but the more a person engages with life, the longer the film gets. If you use your eyes right—the eyes being like the camera lens—the film inside you expands so that it can hold more images. Some people blow up pictures they like and hang them on their walls. But believe me: the day will come when you'll be able to see your picture inside the person who loves you. On this point I think Fairuz was way ahead of her time. So if you don't believe what I'm saying, you can at least believe her, since you love all her songs! One of them goes something like this:

'Open up!' she said,
knocking on my chest's door.
She wanted to see if my heart
was there any more.

"Boy, that woman hits the nail on the head!"

. . .

"I've heard you say, 'All Fairuz's songs are so wonderful, I wish I'd come across just one that's no good so that I can stop being so crazy about her. But what can I say? She's perfect! So do you think she's perfect because I love her, or because her songs are so amazing?'"

. . .

"Uff, we got off the subject again! What I wanted to say was that we aren't just cameras. We're dark rooms, too, in a sort of a way. When I went next door today to ask about Saleh marrying Lamis, I saw Randa as a little girl, the way she was the first time we met. So for a moment I thought of coming right back home again. They're identical, you know."

. . .

"I think we need to start getting ready for the wedding right away. It would be awful to let the day take us by surprise, even though we've been waiting for it forever. Isn't it strange the way weddings always creep up on us?"

. . .

"And you know why it happens? It's because we don't trust the world any more. We've trained ourselves not to expect good things so that when they happen, we can experience the pleasure of feeling awed and amazed."

. . .

"Now, I'm no philosopher. You've been telling me that for a long time. But I wanted to say that I hadn't been seeing things clearly. It's like, my lenses had had a lot of dust on them. But now I'm another Amna. I don't know whether I'm better than the old one or not. But I think I might be because, even though you hardly say anything lately, I get this feeling you love me more now."

Amna, super-neighbor

A LOT HAD CHANGED. AND so had my sister and I.

Without warning, my sister had given up half her girl-friends so that she could spend more time with Amna. Since this narrowed the gap between us in terms of how many friends we had, it gave my mother the impression that I was less isolated than I had been before, even though, actually, nothing had changed.

By some miracle, I got into a lot less hot water with my mom than I always had before, since now she always knew where she could find me—at Amna's house.

My sister and I would wait for her at the front gate when it was time for her to come home from the rehab center where she worked as a supervisor. Since she had a degree in psychology, she must have been a perfect fit for the job. She would come around the corner with a sad look on her face, but the minute she saw us, she'd flash that signature smile of hers.

It took a long time for me to realize how much distress she kept buried inside.

"Nothing hurts more than to see a child suffer," she confided. "Imagine seeing a child you know will never walk, who'll never have any sort of a predictable future."

Sometimes our mother would tell us to go out and play, and we'd do what she'd told us, not because she'd asked us to, but because Amna hadn't objected to her request. If Amna didn't object, this was our cue to give her some time alone with our mom. Yet even then, we wouldn't go far. Instead, we'd sit in the doorway, or rest against the two palm trees in Amna's courtyard. My sister would sit under the little one and I'd sit under the big one, our ears pricked for orders from our mother.

"It's hard to keep standing tall when you see this sort of thing," we heard Amna say.

Amna had to go often to hospitals to meet with wounded children and talk their families into placing them under special care.

"It kills you to know that so many children will never see the sun again."

Children whose eyes had been put out by bullets caused her torment. This sort of injury was getting more and more frequent, and there were moments when she'd start talking as if she were somewhere else.

She said, "When I walk down the street, I keep looking around for their eyes. I think to myself: maybe one of them fell here, or there, and I freak out over the colors that are spattered all over some of the walls, thinking they might be the kids' eyes. Well, last night I dreamed they'd brought us some glass eyes. There were green ones, blue ones, brown ones, hazel ones, and black ones. Some were small and some were big. But they were dead, of course. I was horrified, and I thought: maybe they gouge out some of the kids' eyes, suck the life out of them, and then give them back! One of the kids suggested that they all close their remaining eye and then pick one of the glass eyes off the table. We said no. But they started to cry, and some of them shouted, 'But that's fair!' So we went ahead and let them. But it turned into a nightmare when the kids opened their eyes and we saw a green eye next to a black one, a hazel eye next to a blue one, and that sort of thing. At first they thought it was funny, but then all of a sudden they burst into tears as though they'd met up with little monsters that had been living inside them. I kept my cool as well as I could, and we gathered up the eyes again and took the children out to the hall. But I woke up more scared than ever.

"I mean, really: what do you do when a seven-year-old girl starts screaming all of a sudden, 'These are dead eyes! I want my real ones! I want them now! Now!' and then falls down in front of you, her limbs shaking out of control?"

Saleh was just two months old when Amna's husband Jamal was arrested, and curfews were becoming more and more frequent. So there was plenty to worry about. In any case, one day my mother sat staring at the window that opened onto Amna's courtyard. She stared at it for so long, we started to think there must be somebody standing outside, but that only she could see whoever it was.

"What is it?" I asked.

She didn't answer.

I asked her again, and this time she heard me. "I'm going to turn this window into a door," she said. "That way it will be easier for us to get to her house, and for her to get to ours."

By this time we'd grown up a little and had stopped fighting so much over which of us was Lamis. The fights had started when we decided that Lamis's name was prettier than mine. Then we'd started fighting over Saleh, who had a crush on my sister, and there was a never-ending battle over which of us would take care of him. I could tell she was interested in him too, since her circle of friends had shrunk, and a single boy who lived next to al-Maghrebi's corner store had replaced four girls who'd been her bosom buddies before.

I admit, Saleh liked her the most. I have no idea how he could tell us apart. But when he was old enough to find his tongue, his favorite question was, "When will Lamis be back?"

When he came around asking for her, I'd say, "I'm Lamis."

"No," he'd say. "You're the *other* Lamis."

This question of his caused all sorts of complications in Lamis's life. As soon as my mom heard it, she'd yell at me, "Go find that stinker of a sister of yours and bring her here right now!"

"Randa, you mean?"

"No, Lamis! Are you trying to drive me crazy?"

Then I'd see a sly grin creep onto his face. He'd figured out the easiest, quickest way to get her to come home without lifting a finger.

He hadn't figured it out overnight, of course. He'd gotten lost twice when he went out trying to find her, and the third time we thought we'd never find *him*. Every time we tracked him down we'd ask him, "What brought you here of all places?" And his answer would be, "I was looking for Lamis!"

One day he stood at our door calling her name while she was talking to her crush, Samer. "What do you want?" she snapped, and he blurted out, "I love you, Lamis. I love you!"

She didn't speak to me for a whole week after that. She was convinced I'd put him up to it. "Where on earth would a boy his age get the idea to say something like that unless somebody else had put the words in his mouth?" she demanded.

I swore I'd had nothing to do with it, but she didn't believe me. Then finally, a few days later, I realized that the person who'd been embarrassed wasn't her, but Samer, since other boys in the neighborhood had started taunting him, saying, "What's with you, anyway? People are dying, and you're thinking about girls?"

As if that wasn't bad enough, Saleh escalated the situation even more a few days later.

When he saw that asking about Lamis wasn't bringing her around any more, he resorted to more extreme measures. One day my mother brought the tea over to Amna's house so that we could drink it there. Nadia was taking a nap, but Saleh came to join us. When my mother had finished pouring the tea into the glasses, Saleh took one, my mother took one, and Amna took one. But when I reached out to take mine, he shrieked, "No! That one's for Lamis!" When Amna insisted that I take it, he rushed over to grab it before I could. So now he was holding a glass of hot tea in each hand. My mother pleaded with him to put them down, but he refused, and took a few steps back. His hands were smarting, and pretty soon tears were streaming down his cheeks. But we didn't dare go near him for fear that he'd spill hot tea on himself.

Neither Amna nor my mother drank her tea, and I just sat there shaking like a leaf, as if I'd been the cause of it all. As for Saleh, he went on holding onto both glasses until Lamis got home.

That night, my mother lit into my sister with a fury, swatting her with everything she could get her hands on. "I'm Randa! I'm Randa!" she screamed. But my mother just went on beating her until she was so worn out, she slumped against the wall. She pressed her back against it so hard, it seemed as though she was the one holding it up and that if she had moved, it would have collapsed and brought the whole house—or even the whole world—crashing down with it. In one of her rare moments of despair, she cried, "Lord, what have I done to deserve this load of worries? I've got a husband in prison, two sons on the run, and two daughters that I can't control or even tell apart!"

My sister had no idea what had happened that day. She was bound to find out about it sooner or later, but my mother didn't say a word to her about what Saleh had done, and neither did I. I guess I was afraid that if I did, she might gloat over the fact that he liked her and not me.

We'd figured out easily enough that Amna's husband Jamal was in the same situation as our dad. As for our two brothers, they bickered all the time. Each of them would talk up his own organization and diss the other's—as if they'd forgotten that both of their heads were being targeted by the same bullets. My mother would try to break up the argument, saying, "Look: Israel's out to kill you whether you're with Hamas, Jihad, the PLO, the PFLP, or the DFLP, whether you support the resistance or not, and whether you're for or against Abu Ammar. If you open the window to see what's going on outside, you might die from sniper fire, and whether you're walking down the street or at home in bed, a rocket might fall on your head. So for the life of me, I can't figure out what you two are fighting over!"

Gone were the days when our mother would remark to Amna with a side glance in our direction, "You're looking bright-eyed and bushy-tailed this morning. So, did the engineer come around last night?"

If Amna—who was still just a bride in our eyes even since having Saleh—giggled without answering the question, this would tell our mother that 'the engineer' had slipped in

39

for a visit the night before. My sister, knowing why Amna had giggled, would giggle, too. "What was so funny?" I'd demand as soon as she and I were alone. "It's not polite to laugh for no reason!"

"Some day you'll get it, and when you do, you'll laugh at yourself for not getting it before!"

"What?"

"Oh, nothing."

The time came when Lamis started having to trail Samer from one checkpoint to another to make sure he was all right. Most of the time she would just watch him from a distance, her thirteen-year-old eyes filled with terror. But if her warnings were drowned out by the sound of gunfire, or if he disappeared into a cloud of tear gas, she would come out of her hiding place. This sort of thing happened so many times that some people started calling her jokingly "the Palestinian rapid intervention forces." But one day she put her mockers to shame when she managed to hoist him onto her back and whisk him away from al-Mintar checkpoint, where soldiers had rushed out either to arrest him or to finish him off.

So suddenly Lamis was a heroine. Proud now to be her sister, I didn't dare try to steal the limelight from her, and for a long time I avoided getting into arguments with her over her name.

Meanwhile, Saleh announced to her, "I love you because you're brave."

*

One day Lamis came home from school to find a picture of Samer plastered to our front door. Above it somebody had written in bold black letters: Martyred.

After that she got so unbearably sad that one day I said to her, "Lamis, if you'd like me to be you for a couple of days, or three, or however many, I will. That way you can rest from your grief for a little while."

"I'd been wanting to say the same thing to you," she told me. "You seem even sadder than I am, because you don't cry."

Even martyrs don't grow up that fast

"NO, YOU COULDN'T POSSIBLY HAVE grown up this much."

. . .

"Are you telling me that when martyrs die, they turn into children again?"

. . .

"Did I tell you that? I don't think so! I told you that little children turn into birds in heaven. As for martyrs, they're the beautiful birds of this world. You know why? Because of all people, they're the ones who love freedom the most. They hear it calling, and they go after it. And because it loves them, it goes on playing tag with them. It soars high and swoops low, and they go soaring and swooping after it. They look for it everywhere, not knowing that it's hidden inside their own bodies.

"But the soldiers know it. That's right. The soldiers at checkpoints, in helicopters, and inside tanks, they all know the secret. So do the snipers stationed in their towers. It's that simple. They don't aim at us to kill us. No, they aim at us to kill the freedom that's hidden inside us, the freedom that we keep chasing all our lives. You get me?"

. . .

"Saleh! Saleh! Uff, he's gone back to sleep again! Lord, do I have to keep shouting in their ears to get them to wake up?"

. . .

"Saleh!"

. . .

"What are you saying, Jamal? How can I let him go on sleeping? We've got a million things to do. Do you realize what it means to have a wedding? It means getting everything ready down to the last detail so that people won't think badly of you. Saleh has to get up so that we can go buy him a suit. It's got to fit him just right, and I can't take his measurements when he's lying down. Do you remember what happened when I did that last month so that I could get him a pair of pajamas? I went and bought them, and by the time I got back, he was taller than he had been when I left the house! And that's in spite of the fact that the one I bought that day was more than twice the size of the one I'd gotten him the time before that. You told me I just hadn't taken his measurements right. But when I exchanged it for a bigger one, the one I exchanged it for was too small, too."

. . .

"No, no, I can't do that. By the time I get back, the boy will have gotten taller and broader, I swear to God. I'm not complaining, of course. Thank goodness he's growing so well! But I'm not going to spend all day running back and forth between here and all the clothing stores in town.

"The storekeeper said to me, 'This is the largest size we've got, Ma'am.' 'Well,' I said to him, 'don't you have any men's pajamas?' And he told me that was the only kind they sold in the first place. I went all over Gaza City that day, and every pair of pajamas I brought home was way too small. I put up with that situation, but I won't be able to handle it if it happens with a wedding suit.

"Saleh!"

. . .

"Mustafa, you're the groom's maternal uncle, and you'll have to go with the other men of the family to ask for the girl's hand."

. . .

"What's happened to you? You've never left me on my own before, and now you're telling me to go by myself? It used to be that all I had to do was whisper, and you'd be right there. In fact, sometimes you'd be right there even before I whispered. I know you're tired. You've been tired all your life! But that's no reason to play possum on me."

. . .

"You're all I've got, Mustafa. You're the groom's uncle, and he's crazy about you. Get up, now, and tell him to get up, too. I've got to take him with me to buy the suit. Getting married is no joke. And then there's the wedding dress. Oh Lord, how could I have forgotten? Where's my head? I'm so busy thinking about a suit for my son that I forget all about the dress for the bride who's going to be my daughter!"

"I won't be gone long, you hear? Fifteen minutes to half an hour, max. I've got to consult Randa. She might have an opinion on the matter, and she can ask Lamis, too. Maybe she's got a certain kind of wedding dress in mind. After all, she's been waiting for this day for a long time now. So rather than me going around looking for one, not knowing what she'd like and what she wouldn't, we can go buy one together.

"I had to go looking for my wedding dress all by myself, since you were somewhere else, Jamal, and we were separated by a million checkpoints and patrols, and the various areas of Palestine were zoned off from each other."

. . .

"Of course, none of that is any different now. The only thing that's changed is that I got pregnant and had a baby, then I got pregnant again and had another baby, so that now I've got Saleh and Nadia!"

. . .

"People were saying we couldn't have a wedding if the bride and groom were in two different places, especially with all those soldiers stationed in between. I said, 'I've seen brides cross checkpoints while soldiers watched them from behind sandbags and from inside tanks. And I'm going to do what they did.' Well, I tried. I put on my white gown and went out there, but they sent me back. An Israeli soldier yelled at me in broken Arabic, 'Weddings no allowed!'

46

"'So what *is* allowed, then?' I yelled back. 'You even forbid funerals when you get the chance! You don't want to let us have processions anywhere, whether in our weddings or our funerals!'

"I waved to you on the other side of the checkpoint, you waved back, and we were separated. I cried for three days straight. Then you sent word to me saying, 'You stay where you are. I'm coming to you.'

"'No, please!' I begged. 'Anything but that! Do you want them to kill you? You remember Umm Muhammad, the lady I told you about? I'd gone to her house to congratulate her because her son was getting married that day. When she came to the door she was trilling and singing. Then she started to cry, and I thought to myself: those don't seem like tears of joy to me. As if she'd heard what I was thinking, the woman standing next to me explained, 'Her son was martyred a couple of hours ago.' Two hours before his wedding—imagine! Couldn't they have waited a little longer? I mean, what would have happened if they'd killed just one person less that day? Would that have wiped out the killing fields they've been watering with bullets and bombs and guarding with war planes for the last fifty years and more? Would they have felt so guilty that they couldn't sleep right because they hadn't murdered as many people as they were supposed to?

"So I told you I didn't want you to come. People tried to reassure me. 'Don't worry,' they said. 'We'll bring him in an ambulance.'

"And how was that supposed to keep me from worrying? Don't they search ambulances, too? Don't they fire at them, too?

"'We'll find a way,' they told me.

"I remember how close you were to the checkpoint, Jamal, and but for the mercy of God, you would have met the same fate as that other groom did, and I would have been a widow even before I got married.

"One day we were talking over the phone, and all of a sudden you got quiet on the other end. 'Hello? Hello?' I said, about to panic. Then, after what felt like an eternity, you said, 'Now why hadn't I thought of that before? Would you be willing to marry a martyr?'

"'Are you crazy?' I shouted. 'I want you alive! Alive, you hear?'

"'Well, martyrs are alive, too, aren't they?' you replied.

"'Well, yeah,' I conceded, 'but I want you alive the way you are right now. Not "alive" the way a martyr is.'

"'Don't worry, don't worry. I'm not going to let them make you wait any longer. By tomorrow evening we'll be together. Put your dress on, your white dress, and wait for me.'

"I told my brother Mustafa what had happened, and all he could say was, 'Has your fiancé lost his mind? They'll kill him!'

"Well, anyway, I waited, and I waited, but no you. Then finally somebody came and told me you were in the hospital, in Gaza Central Hospital. So I went in to take off the wedding dress, and he said to me, 'He wants you to come the way you are.'

"I started to cry and cry, as if I'd lost you. When I got to the hospital, I wrapped my arms around you and my dress got all bloody, but for some strange reason you were smiling as though nothing had happened.

"What in God's name are you smiling about? I wondered. Damn it all! I mean, is this the time to be grinning?

"That's when you told me I'd inspired you with the idea of coming inside a coffin. Everybody had been standing around you at the checkpoint and crying. Of course, they weren't crying out of grief, but because they were so scared for you!

"The soldiers weren't buying it, of course, and wanted to see what was inside the coffin. When they were told this wouldn't be possible, they said, 'All right, then, everybody step back.' Then a soldier came up to the coffin, unsheathed his bayonet, and rammed it between the cracks in the wood until it sank into your flesh. When he didn't hear a scream, he stepped away. But then something brought him back again. He thrust the bayonet into the coffin again, only in a different spot this time, making sure it had gone in as far as it would go before pulling it out.

"When he came away the second time, he plunged the bayonet into a sandbag. Everyone came to the horrified realization of what had happened, and their horror intensified when, in the dim light, they saw traces of blood on the bag.

"Did the soldier see it, too? Did he realize that his bayonet had sunk into the flesh of a living being? Or had that never occurred to him? Had he taken pleasure in tormenting a dead man in his coffin the way he might take pleasure in tormenting a pregnant woman by forcing her to deliver her baby at a checkpoint?

"Either way, you didn't scream. And instead of bringing you to me where I'd been waiting for you, they came and brought me to you in the hospital, where you'd been waiting for me.

"Tell me now—how many grooms would be able to bear something like that for their bride? And you ask me why I love you so much, or why I can't bear to be apart from you."

. . .

"Saleh!"

. . .

"For goodness' sake!"

. . .

"Well, then, I'm out of here. I'm going to buy a suit, even if it's nothing but a pair of shorts with a short-sleeved jacket!"

So we can buy the wedding dress

"I CAME SO THAT YOU and the bride and I could go buy the wedding dress together," Amna explained. "She should get to pick it out herself, don't you think?"

"Yes, she should," I agreed.

"But while I was on my way over here, I heard Abu Antar had been martyred, so I decided to go offer my condolences to his family."

"You mean Mustafa al-Ramlawi?" I asked, shocked.

"I'm not sure," Amna admitted. "I just knew him as Abu Antar."

"Who on earth would have killed Abu Antar?" I demanded. The minute I opened my mouth, I realized how naive my question was.

"Seriously, Randa? Who do you think? He was walking past Mafraq al-Shuhada checkpoint when a shell came right at him, a tank shell, and blew his face off. Nobody could even recognize him afterward. The only way they were able to identify him in the end was by his clothes. Imagine having to identify somebody from his clothes, and not his face?"

"God have mercy on him," I murmured. I conjured his image: a fortyish-looking man who used to go around barefoot, his clothes falling apart. He'd make the rounds of the camp's vegetable stalls with a burlap bag on his back and stuff it with fruit that had gone bad.

"So," she went on, "I thought I've got to go pay my respects, since maybe nobody else will. I asked where his house was, and they told me he'd lived alone in one room, and that sometimes he'd be away for days at a time. One woman said to me, 'Are you a relative of his?' 'No,' I told her. Then she said, 'I'm so sorry for your loss!' Imagine, she was comforting me! Granted, he wasn't all there upstairs, but he had the sense never to hurt anybody. I asked the lady where the funeral procession would start, and she said, 'From the hospital, from al-Shifa Hospital.' So I went over, and I got there just in time. There were so many people, I figured somebody important must have died or been martyred. Anyway, I asked somebody where Abu Antar's funeral procession was, and he said, 'This is it.' Oh, God, Randa, I cried! I thought: well, something's right with the world after all. Here was this man I was afraid nobody would remember, and all those people turned out for his funeral. So, then, I thought to myself: we're destined to survive—we Palestinians, I mean. If we weren't, they would have beaten us a hundred years ago."

"I found out that the soldiers had held his body for hours. They said he'd been trying to plant an explosive device at the checkpoint!"

52

"Abu Antar? You've got to be kidding. You'd have to be crazy to believe a thing like that!"

"Anyway, when the funeral procession started moving, I walked behind it. There were thousands of people there, I swear to God. Thousands! They marched from al-Shifa Hospital to al-Nusayrat Camp, and from the camp to his house. When we got there, there were lots of people crying over him, and like I said before, I knew for sure now that there was something right with the world after all. They held prayers for him in the camp's big mosque. Then they went to the Martyrs' Cemetery, and I followed them there.

"When I got to the cemetery, I remembered that I'd been on my way to see you. Then I thought: since the cemetery's near my house, I should pass by to check on the men. So I went over, thinking they might have woken up. But no—they were conked out, just the way I'd left them. So I tiptoed out again. After all, you never know what might happen when people wake up. A mother might wake her son up and say, 'Go buy me a kilo of potatoes,' and five minutes later he's a martyr. You remember Samir Alaywi? He didn't go out to get potatoes for his mother—he was a father with seven daughters and a son. He went out to distribute invitations for his brother Muhammad's wedding, but he didn't make it home alive. You know . . ."

She paused.

"What was I saying? Oh, yeah. You know more than I do, though. Aren't you a journalist?"

I was about to tell her that I hoped to be a journalist some day, but that so far my dreams were too big for my little head.

Then she said something that took me by surprise. "I know you're a writer, and that some day you're going to publish the things you write."

"Who told you that?"

"Come on now, Randa. Your Auntie Amna gets around more than you think she does!"

When I begged her to tell me, she swore me to silence. Once she was satisfied that my oath was sincere, she paused for a bit, her eyes still searching mine. Finally she whispered, "Lamis."

"Lamis?" I said, trying to sound shocked. "But I'm Lamis!"

"Do you think I wouldn't recognize Lamis when I see her? Or that she'd hide something from me? I mean, she's about to become my daughter-in-law!"

Then, looking around, she asked, "Is she home?"

"No," I said. "She went out."

Grandma's voice came from a room in the back. "Who are you talking to?"

"Oh, I'm just talking to myself, Grandma."

"Poor thing. Where's your mind gone, girl?"

My mother, seeing us from the other side of the dirt enclosure, came up to us and said, "Amna, what are you doing standing in the doorway? Come in!"

Amna came in, and I closed the door behind us. My mother led us back to the room whose window had been turned into a door that opened onto Amna's side yard.

"Go make us some tea," my mother said to me. But before I'd gotten out of my chair, she changed her mind.

"That's all right," she told me. "You stay. I'll do it."

At some point my mother had started to realize that I was the only person Amna was really comfortable talking to. This pleased her, actually, and whenever Amna and I went out together, I'd detect a happy, peaceful look on my mother's face.

"With Amna I know you'll be all right."

My mother often came along with us on our outings, so she knew that the places we went to most were martyrs' wakes.

"A duty is a duty," Amna used to say to me. "These people shouldn't feel they're alone after losing somebody they love. There's nothing harder than losing a son, or a daughter, or a brother, or a husband, or anybody dear to you for that matter. The loss itself is bad enough, but what makes it even worse is the timing. It comes exactly when you expected it to—since there isn't a single moment when you don't expect it. But it always takes you by surprise. You know what I mean?"

"Would you mind if I wrote that down?"

"Wrote what down?"

"What you said just now."

"Oh, I see what you're up to!" Then, after a pause, "Is that the sort of thing a person would write down?"

She stole a hard-to-interpret glance over at her yard. Then she went back to talking to me as though the house she'd just looked at wasn't even hers.

"Is Lamis here?" she asked.

"No, she went out."

"Really? Didn't she know I was coming?"

"I forgot to tell her."

"You forgot! Randa, is that the sort of thing a person forgets?"

"Sorry."

"Okay, well, your mom—have you brought up the subject with her?"

"You know, it's fine with my mom. She always says, 'Where could we find a groom better than Saleh? And where could we find nicer folks than you all?' But sometimes she thinks about my dad, and my brother, and me, and she says, 'Is it right to have a wedding when the bride's father is in prison and her brothers are on the run? We're going to be so busy crying over them that we won't have the energy to be happy for the bride and groom.'"

"She's right," Amna conceded. "But look at me. My situation is about as bad as they get. But I always say: we don't know what tomorrow will bring. So we've got to keep going and do what we've got to do, you know."

"Yeah, I know. But some people aren't as brave as others."

"That's true."

My mother brought the tea in and set it down. Then she turned to leave.

"Why don't you have tea with us?" Amna asked her.

"I'm busy. I'll be back after I've finished the laundry."

"And why doesn't Randa help you? Or Lamis? After all, she's old enough to be married herself."

"God bless them," murmured my mother as she left the house without a backward glance.

When my mother was gone, Amna whispered, "Well, at least I reminded her! That ought to get us halfway toward making it official."

I nodded.

"Look, we're late getting out today, and Lamis isn't here. And if you want to know the truth, what happened to Abu Antar has really gotten me down. I mean, I'm sure he's more comfortable now than he was before. But wouldn't there have been a better way to relieve him of his suffering than to kill him off with a tank shell?"

She paused.

"Damn it all. Damn it all," she kept saying.

Wanting to console her, I whispered, "Maybe God wanted to honor him by letting him die as a martyr."

"Ya think?"

I nodded.

Then, without finishing her tea, Amna shot up out of her chair. "Where are you going?" I asked, startled. "It's still early."

"They'll start to worry about me," she explained. Gesturing toward her little girl, whose whole life had been colored by

57

her mother's grief, Amna added, "It's gotten dark, and as you can see, Nadia's tired."

Seeing her on her way to the front entrance, I invited her to go out the side door that joined our sitting room to her inner courtyard, hoping she might go back to her old habit. But, as I knew she would, she declined, saying, "If I leave that way, I feel as though I just stayed at home and didn't go anywhere. But if I go out the front, I can say I went on a visit."

I escorted her to the door, and watched her until she disappeared.

When I went back into the room where we had been sitting, I could see her through the window-turned-door. I heard her key turn in the lock. She looked in my direction, waved, and smiled before disappearing inside.

I smiled back, but that didn't stop tears from streaming down my cheeks.

What are they bombing today?

I WAS ON MY WAY home from Umm Jawad's house one day when I heard rockets exploding. "So what are they bombing today?" I started asking people. A boy was about to tell me, but before he could get the answer out, I said, "I know. Don't tell me. They're bombing the Martyrs' Cemetery, aren't they?"

"That's right, Auntie," he said.

He was a beautiful, sweet boy, just like you when you were little, Saleh. "God keep you for your mama!" I said to him.

I stood there just thinking about him for a while. Then suddenly I popped out of my reverie. My God! I thought to myself. What are you doing, Amna? And I came running.

Didn't I tell you no place was safe any more? You remember Mustafa al-Ramlawi—Abu Antar? Well, they killed him at Mafraq al-Shuhada checkpoint. I can't help thinking to myself: if they'll stoop to the level of killing people as harmless as Mustafa—God have mercy on him—then what's to keep them from killing the whole lot of us?

"Even the Martyrs' Cemetery isn't safe any more!" I said to myself. Six rockets hit it. And why? Did you hear that boom? It shook all of Gaza. Really, nowhere's safe any more.

A little while ago Aziz passed by. You know Aziz, right? He said good morning and asked me if I needed anything. "No, sweetie, bless your heart," I said to him. "Just take care of yourself."

"Well, anyway," he added, "I won't be far away."

"So," I asked him, "are you all going to dig new graves?"

He nodded. "The guys'll be here soon."

That boy's obsessed with digging graves. He always says to me, "You know, Auntie Amna, they kill more of us off every day, so we should always have some graves ready. A few days ago they dropped a rocket that left three dead. Then, when people gathered to save people in the car and on the street, they flew over and left seven more dead and fifty wounded. Somebody had lost a leg, so they went looking for it and found what they thought was it. But when he saw it, the man screamed, 'How many right legs do you think I have, damn it?' It was a massacre, Auntie. We spent two days scraping flesh off walls and ceilings. We managed to gather it all into bags, but we knew there was no way we'd be able to tell which body parts belonged to who. So I said, 'Why don't we just bury them all in one grave?' But they rejected the idea. Now tell me, Auntie: don't you think that would have been better? Why should we make martyrs go looking all over the place for their body parts on Resurrection Day?"

I didn't know what to say to him. Then he went on, "You know what I hope for, Auntie?"

"What's that, my dear?"

"I hope for the day when we don't have to dig extra graves any more."

"Well," I stammered, "we don't have any say in that. But if we're going to have to dig graves even before people die, then—though I'm sure you don't want me to tell you this—make the graves big enough to give the martyrs lots of room. You don't want them to feel cramped in there. And make them deep enough that the rockets they drop on the cemetery won't get to them."

When I said that, he burst out laughing as if it was the funniest thing he'd ever heard. "Don't worry, Auntie, when I dig a grave, I do it as if it were for me."

"Don't think that way!"

"I wish I didn't need to."

He took a few steps away. Then he turned back toward me. There was a glare from the sun behind him, but I could still see his face. I rubbed my eyes, thinking: this can't be. But when I opened them again, his features were still sharp, and I heard him saying to me, "But if I do die, don't forget to come by and talk to me. People are so worried about who's going to die, they forget to think about the ones who are already dead. Of course, they're right to be worried. I mean, look at me: I'm busy all the time trying to take care of people who are about to die."

*

The first time I saw Aziz digging, I said, "What are you doing here?"

"I'm digging graves," he said.

"And what do you think you're going to find in martyrs' pockets?" I asked him.

"Don't you know?"

"No," I said. I thought he was a grave robber, like the ones we hear about or see in movies.

"Don't worry," he reassured me. "People who rob martyrs don't need to dig up their graves. You know why?"

"Why?"

"They rob them before they die. Then they pile lots of dirt on top of them so they'll never come back. You see what I mean?"

"Yeah, I see," I said. And I started to like him.

He started laughing right there in the cemetery. "Lower your voice," I cautioned him.

"Don't worry," he said cheerily. "The people buried here love laughter more than anybody else, since they loved life more than anybody else."

He scrambled effortlessly over to me among the tombstones as though he'd been doing it forever. He didn't even need to look where he was going.

By this time I'd really taken to him.

I remarked, "We only learn life's lessons when we work, whether the work we do is digging graves or building mansions."

One time when I saw him working so hard, I said, "Listen, Aziz, tomorrow's another day. You can finish that job in the morning."

I was tired myself, of course. I wanted to go to sleep, and I wanted him and his buddies to do the same, but it looked as though they were going to go on digging all night.

Aziz's answer was, "Can you guarantee they aren't going to kill anybody tonight?"

"No," I admitted.

"Well, then," he said, "bear with us."

It was hot as blazes that night, as though the sun hadn't gone down. In any case, half an hour later, an F-16 came roaring overhead and dropped a rocket that weighed three thousand kilos. It killed Salah Shahada and six members of the Matar family alone. And the day of the funeral it rained three times—in July, of all things (it never rains in July!). We couldn't believe our eyes.

Another time Aziz said to me, "I've started to scare myself, Auntie. I keep getting sadder and sadder."

"Why is that, my boy?" I asked.

"I've started to sense the moment when I have to leave my friends or get out of bed to dig new graves. I'll get a feeling that more death is on its way, but I don't know which path it's going to take, so I don't know how to warn people, and that kills me. Then I dug a grave today, and the shovel was going in a lot more easily than usual."

He took me by the hand and led me over to a spot where there were three graves side by side. Pointing, he said, "Do you see how the two graves on the outside are full of rocks? So why is it that the one in the middle doesn't have any rocks in it at all? It's pure soil."

"I have no idea!" I confessed.

"It gives me a weird feeling!" he said.

And two days later he was martyred.

Before it happened, he told his friends at al-Mintar checkpoint to go on ahead of him.

"Where?" they asked him.

"To see Auntie Amna. Ask her to lead you to the grave Aziz told her about."

I'm always at a loss . . .

. . . WHEN I THINK ABOUT THE incredible things people say. Some of them are elderly, uneducated folks who haven't had a day of schooling in their lives. Then out of the blue, they come out with some gem of wisdom so profound that no educated person could have said anything half as earthshaking, and I wonder how it can happen. But as amazing as it is, I wouldn't believe it if somebody told me these people had heard these things somewhere, memorized them, and saved them up for this or that situation. I mean, sayings like these would be hard to memorize. Besides, it's pretty unlikely that people would talk about things like these unless they'd experienced them firsthand. In other words, they aren't the sort of thing you could just dictate to somebody and have him regurgitate it an hour later, much less years later.

People who talk this way make me think of characters in a novel. A novelist doesn't put down everything a character thinks about all day long. Instead, he has his characters say the best, most important things. So maybe we come to love a character in a novel the way we come to love a poet. We know, for example, that a poet does ordinary things like eat and drink and watch television, and that he dreams, gets happy and sad and angry, listens to music, and even pees. But we push this knowledge to the back of our heads so that all we see of the poet is his poetry. That's how he becomes "a poet" in our eyes, just the way a person becomes a character in a novel.

When I read Ghassan Kanafani's novel *Umm Saad*, I kept thinking: where on earth would a woman like this have picked up so much wisdom? Yeah—Umm Saad is the perfect example. Then I started wondering too: what happens with Umm Saad outside Kanafani's novel? Does she get sick? Does she get sad? Does she have mood swings? What all did she do in her lifetime, outside that novel's ninety pages?

I mean, I know a woman like Umm Saad has to be wonderful. But she might not have been as wonderful twenty, thirty, or forty years earlier. She might have been like me, like us. Even if she was, the question remains: why did Kanafani put only the best parts of her in the novel? Was it because when he met her, she took a liking to him because he made her think of her son Saad and, as a result, she poured out her emotions and thoughts as though she were talking to herself? Or is it just that novels are only novels if they're like this, and their characters can only be proper characters if they're this way—saying exactly what's supposed to be said, and nothing else, at just the time when it should be said, then disappearing and reappearing, only to say what's supposed to be said in some other situation?

How many pages would Kanafani have had to write if he'd wanted to describe Umm Saad's life down to the last little detail? Would we have loved her as much if we'd read the thousand- or two-thousand-page version of her story? Or maybe the reason she's so perfect is just that she's completely present in the moment, whereas the rest of us spend our lives outside the moment.

I swear I'm going to go crazy. I write one article after another and send them off to newspapers, but to this day not a single one of them has gotten published.

A few months ago a journalist said to me, "Children would never think this way, whether they're martyred or not."

"But they do think this way!" I told him. "In fact, they think even more deeply than this. Your problem is that when you read what I've written about other kids and what they've said, you discover that they think better than you do, and that grieving mothers think better than you do. That's because, instead of getting your hands dirty with real life, you go around with your head stuck in a dictionary. Since you own the key to a publishing house, you think you know more than everybody else. What you've forgotten is that the doormat we hide our house key under is the same mat we use to wipe the dirt and mud from the street off our shoes before we come inside."

I figured I'd never be able to publish anything in that newspaper as long as people like him worked there. But as I left the place, I felt strong. In fact, I felt like Superwoman. It was as if I'd had the kind of epiphany that comes to some of the people

I talk to, or to characters in novels. Otherwise, where would I have gotten the idea of the key under the doormat? I'd really put him in his place! I mean, who does he think he is? He thinks he holds the keys to our mouths and our hearts, to what we should and shouldn't say. Who gave him the right to decide how things are supposed to be said and written, anyway? Is he some kind of computerized spelling and grammar checker?

Actually, I'm not sure the spellchecker analogy works as well as the doormat one, and if I were writing a novel, I'd probably chuck it.

But what was I supposed to do now? I'd been collecting little stories. Some I'd heard from other people, some were based on things I'd been through myself, and some I'd clipped out of newspapers. And I kept wondering: what are our authors doing today? Why aren't *they* writing about all these things?

After my argument with that journalist, I decided to scribble down whatever I saw with the idea that some day I might hand my scribblings over to a 'real' writer. I thought: maybe I'll go find Ghassan Kanafani's grave and tell him, "Get up now and write down these poor orphaned stories that nobody pays any attention to! Because if we don't write down our story, you know what's going to happen to it? (Sorry for going on like this, Ghassan, but I know I can talk to you from the heart. I can rant and rave to you without feeling embarrassed, since you're one of us.) Do you know what happens to the stories we don't write down?"

. . .

"I'll tell you what happens to them: they become enemy property."

Whenever a door closed in my face, I'd go knock on Ghassan's, since his was always open.

Last night I saw him in a dream. It made me so happy. He was walking down a street that I recognized, but didn't. It was broad and clean, and it had the sea on both sides of it. At first I followed him from a distance. I didn't dare come right up to him. I realized I was dreaming, and that I was going to wake up. Everything overlapped with everything else, and I heard a voice—it might have been my own— saying, "Where's your nerve, girl? You talk about him night and day, but when he shows up, you run away like a scared little mouse!"

"Me, a scared little mouse?" That made me mad. If I were 'a scared little mouse,' I wouldn't have said what I said to that nasty old journalist.

But then I started to think about how, if I went on this way, I was going to miss out on the chance to meet him.

I looked in his direction. By this time he was way ahead of me. But then I heard him calling me by name. I wondered how he could be sure who I was, since even my mother couldn't tell me and my sister apart.

I took off running toward him, but every time one of my feet touched the ground, the sea on either side of the street rose a little higher.

I heard him calling me again and telling me to hurry. So I sped up, and just when I started to think I'd never catch up with him, I saw him smile and reach out to me. But when our fingertips touched, it turned out that the hand belonged to my sister.

Then I woke up in a fright.

Don't make me laugh!

"PLEASE! WHAT WOULD PEOPLE SAY if they heard me?"

. . .

"I know—we used to meet in secret as husband and wife more than we ever did before we got married. You'd message me to come out of the house and walk in any direction I wanted to, and to let you choose the moment when we'd meet. As I walked, I'd feel as though you were all of Gaza, from north to south, from east to west. 'What's happening to us?' I'd ask. 'How is it that a wife has to arrange trysts with her own husband?'

"And you'd say, 'This is the one good thing about living in hiding. You appreciate being together more when you have to work so hard for it.'

"And that would make me mad. 'What do you mean by that?' I'd demand. 'So you didn't appreciate being with me when we were courting?'

"'No, no!' you'd insist. 'But now that I have to stay in the shadows so much of the time, the light that glows when I'm with you gives the world a meaning beyond the misery we're enduring.'

71

. . .

"You used to take me down long alleyways, to places I'd never even known existed. I'd tell you you were going too far in your security precautions, and you'd say, 'These aren't security precautions—they're marital precautions! Just think—if we got caught together, tongues would be wagging all over Gaza. People would start saying, "Did you hear? We saw a man with his wife!"'

"Then you'd start laughing again. But I'm not going to laugh this time. I can't.

"'You know,' you once said to me, 'my heart used to nearly beat out of my chest at the mere thought that I'd get to see you, and as I followed you from a distance, I'd think to myself: now there's a woman who'd be worth starting a war over if anything came between us! Ironically, though, they started a war first, to keep me from seeing her.'

"I felt so grateful that life's cruelty hadn't hardened your heart toward me. Then—as if you could read my mind—you said, 'You know when a person gives up, Amna? It's when he forgets the people he loves and starts thinking about nobody but himself. He might imagine that his own life is the most important thing in the world when it's nothing but dust and ashes.'

"'For God's sake,' I'd beg you, 'don't get poetic on me and make me cry again!'

"By the way, Randa says we're all poets—or, rather, not that we're all poets, exactly, but that inside each of us there's a poet who comes out when we really come face to face with

72

ourselves. When that happens, we start to glow, and we might say things nobody would ever have heard come out of our mouths otherwise. You remember the movie *Jenin* that was on one of the satellite channels? When that young nurse Hala found out the corpse she was sitting beside in the ambulance belonged to her brother Jaber, who'd been martyred in the camp, she said, 'Sadness isn't tears. Sadness is the ability to keep yourself from crying for somebody else's sake.' In this case, the 'somebody' for whose sake she was keeping herself from crying was her little brother, since she didn't want to shock him with the news of his big brother's death.

"According to Randa, some people have lots of luminous moments like these, while others don't have many at all. Unfortunately, some people only have this kind of experience right before they die. And I believe her. How could I not believe Randa, of all people? But do you know the crazy things that go through that girl's head? Besides the fact that she still insists that her name is Lamis, she talks about sneaking out of Gaza and going to visit the grave of Ghassan Kanafani—that heart-throb of yours! She says she wants to dig his grave open, give him all the stories she's collected, and say, 'In spite of all the death that's in these pages, there's enough life in them to make you jump out of there and go back to writing again!'"

. . .

"You see what a beautiful night it is, Jamal? It's so quiet, it makes me feel as though Gaza must have been liberated a long time ago!"

73

. . .

"Randa keeps on telling me, 'You know, Auntie Amna, somebody like Ghassan Kanafani should get to write at least one novel posthumously. I mean, do you really think he doesn't know what's going on now? He knows more than all the rest of us put together And it tortures him not to be able to write the way he used to.'

"She says, 'Beautiful people whet Death's appetite. And Ghassan is one of the beautiful people.' She says that because they're beautiful, Death senses their presence from the time they're born and starts trying to snatch them up. Sometimes it gets them, sometimes it doesn't. Now, some of the beautiful people hear Death sneaking up on them from the very start. Granted, you're not going to see Annihilation chasing a newborn baby down the streets. But just because you can't see it happening doesn't mean it isn't real. And Ghassan is one of those people who started running really early. "'You see, Auntie Amna,' she says, 'Death has no pity on people like these because they've had no pity on Death.' She tells me they don't run because they're not trying to escape. Rather, it's more like a wild, cutthroat race. The only reason beautiful people become beautiful is that they've managed to rescue the things they love—the things we love, the things Life loves—from Death's clutches. They liberate the rose, the tree, the sparrow's wing. They liberate the horse's neigh, the sun, and the rain. They liberate butterflies, tigers, and gazelles. But if Death catches up with them, it takes back all the beautiful things they've rescued. Do you think this world could still exist if it weren't for the fact that these beautiful people keep snatching its beauty from the jaws of Death?

"Kanafani knew he was living for a struggle that was bigger than he was, and he accomplished what he did in just thirty-six years. Actually, he did it in a lot less time than that. When he saw Death gaining on him, he started writing like mad, and all his writing was done in less than sixteen years. Randa asks me: 'Do you think he did that just because he loved to write? If that were the case, then three-fourths of the world's population would be authors! No, he wrote what he did because he loved Life. Because he loved us. Because he loved me!'"

. . .

"Randa told me that sometimes she goes out in the yard and sees Death flying overhead in an Apache helicopter or an F-16. So she comes running back inside and grabs Kana-fani's books. Then she brings them out and lifts them high and screams, 'You can do anything you want, but you'll never be able to kill these! He beat you, and all of these are ours. Remember?'"

. . .

"You know, Jamal? Sometimes I feel as though Randa looks just like me. In fact, sometimes I feel she's more beauti-ful than I am, even though she thinks I'm more beautiful than she is."

. . .

"Now don't laugh at me! But I said to her once, 'Let's trade places. You be me, and I'll be you.' 'I wish we could,' she said. 'Then I could stop fighting with my sister over that name!'"

"One day I told you Saleh wanted your picture.

"'Why would he want my picture?' you wanted to know. 'I see him whenever I get the chance!'

"I explained to you that he wanted your picture because 'whenever you get the chance' wasn't enough for him. He knew your appearance must be changing all the time. And sometimes I felt the same way, especially at those moments when I needed you, all of you, the way a woman needs the man she loves, and was having troubling conjuring your face. You know?

"Sometimes I feel as though we never had a proper wedding celebration. Now don't get me wrong, I just mean, sometimes I feel as though we were only together twice: when we conceived Saleh before you went to prison, and when we conceived Nadia after you got out. It's as if we'd become nothing but baby-making machines."

. . .

"You think I'm exaggerating? Well, maybe I am. But what I mean is that the occupation has deprived us of a real life together. We might manage to get together now and then, but we need each other a hell of a lot more than that.'

"You told me you'd take a picture of yourself when you got the chance, but added: 'As soon as you've shown it to

Saleh, tear it up. All right? Tell him that this was what his dad looked like on that day. Then, after he's taken a good long look at it, get rid of it.'"

What I didn't tell you was that he wouldn't let me tear them up. Every time I told him I was going to, he'd cry so hard that I'd change my mind. 'Okay, then,' I'd tell him, 'I'll put them away for you. I'll hide them somewhere because the occupation forces are after him, and we don't want them to know exactly what he looks like, because they, as you know . . . .'

"Then he'd snap at me, 'What do you think I am? A little boy?'

"'Of course you're not!' I'd assure him.

"When he closed his eyes, I'd go to the other room, turn on the light, pick up your picture, and get ready to tear it up. But before I could do it, I'd burst into tears. Knowing I'd never be able to do it while I was looking at it, I'd shut my eyes, but that didn't work, either. So I'd get up and turn off the light, hoping that would give me the courage to tear up my sweetheart's picture. I'd be crying so hard that the darkness around me would start to tremble. When the sun came up the next morning, the picture would still be in my hand, and my dress would be black with grief. Then I'd hide it, and when another came in, I'd hide that one, too."

. . .

"Thank God I did that. Otherwise, I don't know what I would have said to Saleh the day he came to me in tears,

77

complaining, 'Since you tore up all his pictures, we haven't got a single one left!'

"I went to my hiding place and got them all out. When I handed them to him, he was so excited he started jumping up and down. It made me think of when you used to throw him up in the air and catch him again . . . throw him up and catch him again . . .

Why are you always late?

"YOU'RE ALWAYS LATE!" AMNA blurted out angrily. "Why is that?!"

"You mean he isn't here?"

"That's right, Randa. He isn't here."

She'd talked to me a lot about Aziz. Once she said, "Since you're like my own daughter, I can't help thinking about your future, and I've decided you need a husband like Aziz. Now to tell you the truth, I've talked to him about the idea, too. I said to him, 'You need a bride as sweet as you are, and I've got the girl for you. Her name is Randa!'"

"Whoa! Take it easy now, Auntie! One of these days I'm going to wake up to find out that I got married without even knowing about it!"

She sidled up to me and, after making sure nobody was within ear shot, she whispered, 'Don't worry. I've gotten a lot older, but I'm not old-fashioned. To this day I still sneak out for secret rendezvous with Jamal. Don't you dare tell anybody, though! They're still after him, you know, and I'd die if I were the cause of some harm coming to him."

All her talk about Aziz had really piqued my curiosity. I'd even jotted down some impressions of him in my notebook. I was curious about him not the way a girl would be curious about a guy, but as an aspiring writer, or as a collector of stories about Palestine.

Amna said, "Sometimes he comes to the cemetery and scans the place to get an idea of how many empty graves there are. I can see he's doing it without his telling me so. Well, one day he didn't find a single empty grave, and he started to cry. He cried like a baby. I took him into my arms and rocked him. He clapped his hands over his eyes, but he still kept on crying, and the tears seemed to be coming from somewhere far, far away. For all I knew, they were coming from the funeral of this land's first martyr—or maybe from Jesus's funeral. His tears seemed tired, like us. So when I rested his head on my shoulders, I don't know if it was his head that I was resting there, or tears that, like us, have been looking for a shoulder to fall on."

"'Oh, God, I'm worn out!' he moaned, as if he were a thousand years old.

"One time he said, 'You know, Auntie Amna, once this occupation's over, I'm never gonna touch a shovel again, not even to plant flowers!'

"'Don't say things like that!' I cried. 'That's just what the occupiers would want! They want us to stop being beautiful and loving beautiful things. Don't give them the satisfaction.'"

She stopped talking for a while. Then she confessed, "To be honest, I don't think he'll hold up till the occupation's over."

It was on account of this comment of hers that I agreed to come meet him. He seemed to give off a special sort of light.

We looked all over for him that day. We passed by all the checkpoints. We searched the main roads. We went down every alleyway and back street we could think of. No luck. Finally Amna suggested, "Why don't we look for him at his house?"

"Do you know where he lives?"

"No."

"How will we look for him there, then?"

"Let's go to the cemetery and follow the light you talked about. That'll get us there."

"Now who you told about the trail of light?"

"Oh, nobody!" she said evasively, like a little girl who's been caught doing something she's not supposed to do.

Wanting to put her at ease again, I quipped. "And what will his mother say when a couple of good-looking dames show up on her doorstep asking about her son?"

"I don't know," Amna rejoined, not skipping a beat, "but it's sure to make her happy!"

"Happy?"

"Yep. Mothers are sort of weird that way. In front of other people they pretend to be put off or uncomfortable if something like that happens. But afterward, they laugh up their sleeves. Take it from me!"

. . .

"You remember how Lamis used to think up nice things to say to me about Saleh—as if I didn't already know how nice he was. She was shy about it, of course, but I was happy to see that he'd grown up enough to catch her eye. I'll be honest—it made me really glad. After all, where would a mother like me find a girl for her son as nice as Lamis? And he was happy, too, of course."

Then she looked over at me and exclaimed, "Now look at me! I'm busy worrying about you and Aziz. But I don't see anybody worrying about me!"

"What do you mean by that?" I asked, taken aback. "You're my best friend!"

"Come on now, Randa! Things have dragged out for way too long. We've got to get those two together, and you promised to talk to your mother about it so that we could get the thing settled. But you haven't done it yet!"

"I haven't forgotten." I said resolutely. "I just haven't been able to find the right time."

"Actually, I could have talked to Lamis directly," she said, softening. "After all, she's old enough to decide for herself what's right for her and what isn't. But protocol is protocol. I hinted to her about it the other day, and I think she got my drift. In fact, I think it made her happy, since she didn't say anything, and well, like they say, 'Silence means yes!' If things go the way I've been hoping, there might be two weddings—Lamis's, and yours."

"So," I demanded suddenly, "is that why you want to marry me to Aziz? Because you think I'm older than Lamis?"

She looked at me with tears in her eyes. "Seriously, Randa? I may have gotten older, but as I've said before, I'm not stuck in the past. I've even begun to wonder if I've lost my mind. I mean, what's gotten into me, that I'd be willing to get so mixed up in this matchmaking game?"

"Since we're at the market, let me get some vegetables. It's been a long time since I cooked them something that's good for their digestive system. The mulukhiya looks great today. See?"

I nodded.

"I'll buy the chicken from somewhere nearer to home so that we won't have to carry it all the way back."

Turning to me, she added, "Why don't you come for lunch today? Maybe he'll surprise us and show up."

"Who?"

"Have you forgotten already? Aziz!"

When I visited Amna a few days later, she was down in the doldrums.

All she could say was, "Why are you always late?"

"What do you mean?" I asked. "We didn't have an appointment, did we? I just dropped by."

"Even so, you're late!" she repeated sourly.

"Did Aziz come and then leave? Or what?"

"He came, and he hasn't left. But you're still late." She started to cry.

I left her and went out to the cemetery. As I roamed the graveyard, I wondered: does a single day go by without somebody being martyred around here?

I scanned the dates engraved on the tombstones. There were only a few days when we hadn't lost somebody—as if Death had taken a little break, but that was all. How could it be so greedy? I couldn't wrap my head around it. It seemed to devour everything in sight without a second thought.

I went walking down the years among those tombstones until I found myself looking at a date that brought me back to the present, or to be more precise, to one day earlier. Above the date there was a big poster and a bouquet of flowers that still hadn't wilted. From behind the flowers, a young man's face on the poster peeked out at me. The face looked familiar. And when I read the name, I burst into tears. It was Aziz.

"Maybe you took it more seriously than I did," I told him guiltily. "Maybe you loved me so much you never wanted to see me, so you decided to cut things short from the start, and left this world. But I hope you did it because you were worried about me, not because you wanted to run away from me!"

Suddenly I jumped up and took off running among the graves. What was happening to me? Had I started talking to dead people?

When I saw Amna again two days later, she told me she'd been furious with me for not making time to meet Aziz. Kissing her on the head, I begged her to forgive me.

She did.

We sat for a long time in a silence that seemed to have descended out of nowhere and spread all around us without our noticing. Then, her voice sounding as though it were coming from some distant place, like the day I saw her for the first time at our door, she commented, "You see, Randa? I go to the market, come home, and cook up a storm. Then after all that, nobody eats a bite. The food's sitting there just the way it was when I put it on the table. I don't even know why I go to the trouble!"

Then she turned to me and said, "If I put out some for you, will you eat?"

I heard her calling

I'D NEVER HEARD HER SOUND like that before. She was all riled up.

"You get up here right now, girl!"

I got going quick, sprinting past the concrete bench and bounding up the stairs that led to the roof of the house. It wasn't even six-thirty in the morning yet.

"What's wrong, Grandma?"

"What's wrong? Why should you even need to ask? Where did you get the coffee you brought home yesterday? Didn't I tell you not to buy it from that scumbag? What does he do with the stuff, anyway—roast it straight over the sun? It broke up my sleep the way Abu al-Abed's cleaver breaks up a leg of lamb!"

"But I didn't buy it from him. I got it from the best shop on Umar al-Mukhtar Street."

"What's it called?"

"I don't know, actually. But I smelled it from the sidewalk, and it made me think of you, so I decided to buy you some. He told me it was one hundred percent Brazilian coffee."

"Brazilian coffee! Who told you I'd want that?"

"Mama said you liked it."

"Well, I liked it fifty or sixty years ago. But when I gave up hope, I started to hate it."

"Nobody hates Brazilian coffee, Grandma."

"Well, *I* do!" She said it so ferociously, I started eyeing her hand to make sure she wasn't about to grab her cane and wallop me with it.

"I don't want any of that stuff in the house. You got that?"

"I got it, Grandma. But can't you tell me the reason?"

"The reason is that it threw me off balance!"

"I don't understand, Grandma. Just talk on my level, will you?"

"Your grandpa, your grandpa! I dreamed about him five times last night!"

"Oh! Well, why didn't you say so from the start?"

"You'd never understand. But what I'm saying is that since I dreamed about him, I know that coffee of yours threw me out of whack. I stopped dreaming about him a long time ago. I sort of boycotted him, you might say. Back when he was writing me from Brazil and telling me he was going to come home, I liked Brazilian coffee. In fact, it was the only kind I drank for a while. The shopkeepers would try to trick me into buying their coffee sometimes by telling me it was from Brazil when it was really from Yemen. But I could tell the difference, because the other coffee didn't make me think of your grandpa. You get me? But when I gave up on him—when he died without coming back like he'd promised he would—I started to feel all

88

creepy whenever I had Brazilian coffee. So I don't drink it any more, you got that? I don't drink it any more!"

I tried to say a word or two in apology, but her hand was sliding in the direction of her cane.

"Don't you say a word," she snapped. "Not a word. You've done enough harm as it is tonight. I dreamed about him, you hear? When that happened, I shot awake to get away from him as fast as I could. He tried again a couple of times, but I was ready for him."

After a pause, she went on, "Has anybody ever told you why people dream, girl?"

"No," I admitted.

"It's because they don't get enough of life. They dream so that they can imagine that they're awake—that they haven't missed anything. And I do the same thing. But dream about him? No way! Even if it means I don't get to live as long. Of course, sometimes we don't have any say in what happens. It looks like I finally got so tired, he slipped into my dream 'with little resistance,' as they say on the news broadcasts. Now, if he'd stopped there, it wouldn't have been so bad. But he had the nerve to tell me, 'You've got to get married, Wasfiya!' 'Me, get married?' I said. 'That's right. And I didn't come see you until I'd found you a real catch.' 'Oh, really!' I yelled. 'So you've even brought the groom along? Wherever he is, you must be out of your mind, man. Do you think I'm still of marrying age?' I mean, I was boiling mad. I screamed, 'Listen, you old geezer. Don't you know I'm all

89

dried up? All you had to do was take a good look at me to figure that out!'

"'Don't you go trying to fool me,' he chuckled. 'When I died, you were as young as could be. And good-looking, too!'

"'Oh, so you saw me before you died? I doubt if you could even remember what I looked like by the time you croaked!'

"'You couldn't have gotten old,' he insisted. 'I just died a few days ago!'

"'A few days ago? What's this bullshit? You've been dead for the last fifty or sixty years!'

"'Don't get morbid on me, woman! If I'd been dead that long, how could I have come all the way from Brazil to Gaza to see you, and then back again, five times in one night?'

"'You knew I didn't want you barging into my dreams. I shut you out over and over again, but you finally wore me out so bad that you could sneak in on me. So if you've still got so much get-up-and-go that you can hop back and forth between Brazil and Gaza five times in one night, why don't *you* marry me?'

"'Me?'

"'Yeah, you! What do you need that I haven't got?'

"'Well, nothing,' he admitted. 'But how can I marry you when you're already my wife?'

"'Oh, right! That wouldn't make any sense, would it?'

"'Now you're talking!'

"'But do you really want me to get married? Are you serious?'

"'Yep,' he said.

"But I know what he meant," my grandma said to me. "I know what he was getting at. There's only one reason he would have come to me five times last night. You know why?"

Before I could reply, she went on, "Well you see, honey—your grandpa's got a yearning!"

"A yearning?"

"That's right. I'm sure of it, and you know why? Since he didn't do a single thing in his life that would have made me sorry he was gone, God punished him by not letting him have any of those big-eyed virgins!"

"I don't understand, Grandma."

"You don't understand? Well, your grandpa used to try every trick in the book if he . . . ."

She stopped talking.

"How old are you?" she asked me.

"Twenty-five, maybe."

"Twenty-five. So, then, you know what kinds of things go on between husbands and wives?"

I nodded.

"What did your grandpa used to do?" she quizzed me.

"Try every trick in the book."

". . . if he wanted me. You get it?"

"I get it."

"So then, why wouldn't he come from Brazil five times in one night?"

After another long pause, I started to get up.

"Sit down," she said. "I'm not finished. How are your brothers and sisters?"

"They're fine," I said. "But things are hard. When the occupation authorities are after somebody the way they're after Baba, you can't help but worry about him, you know. He has to keep his eyes to the ground, and he has to keep them on the sky, too. Some of the airplanes you see, and some of them you don't."

"God be with them."

More silence. I fidgeted. She started talking again.

"You know what your grandpa really wants?"

"What?"

"He wants to take me to where he is. I think he misses me. And I don't think it has anything to do with his not having any big-eyed virgins!"

"Do you miss him too, Grandma?"

"Well, I've got no mind to die just to meet up with him, if that's what you mean!"

"You've got plenty of years ahead of you, Grandma."

"You never know how long you've got left. Don't you know that? But there's something else I want to happen before I'm gone."

"What's that?"

"I haven't lived all these years and gone through all I've gone through just so I can die before I see those occupiers leave with my own two eyes. Do you think I'll be ready to go before I know you, your mama, and your brothers and sisters are going to be all right? Isn't it enough that they robbed me of the chance to make sure your sister, Jamal, Saleh, Amna, Mustafa, and Aziz were going to be okay?"

"You've made me sad, Grandma."

"I wish I could have made you happy."

"It makes me happy just to have you around."

"Hah! Now admit it—you want to run away from me sometimes, don't you? I can feel it."

"Well, I guess so. May I go now?"

"Yes, you may."

"Really?"

"Of course, really. In fact, if you don't get up, I'll shoo you out with my cane."

"Anything but that!"

Then somehow or other, I'm not sure how, I ended up with Amna.

I knew it was you

I KNEW ONLY SOMETHING HUGE, something cataclysmic, would have kept you from coming back to me.

I'd been watching television with Randa and Saleh. We'd been watching it, but not watching it. It was just sort of there in front of us without our paying any attention to it.

I kept thinking: why do we keep it on if nobody's watching it?

For some reason, though, we kept looking at it every now and then. Randa kept asking me, "What do we expect to see on the screen that we haven't already seen with our own eyes?"

Maybe we were just watching it out of habit. After all, we should be humble enough to admit that there are things on television that we haven't seen with our own eyes.

"Besides," she went on, "even if the stuff on TV isn't something we've seen ourselves, it isn't that different from what goes on right here."

She's smart, that girl. You know, if Saleh were even a little sweet on her, I would have tried to get the two of them

95

together, and she would have helped him forget about Lamis. But the heart has its ways!

Sorry—I know I've told you that a million times.

The fact is, she's never left my side. I always feel her hand in mine, and on my forehead. Even when I'm asleep I hear her talking to me. Now I'm going to tell you something strange. I know you're not going to believe it. But when this girl sits next to me at night and puts her palm on my forehead, I sleep like a baby.

I said to her once, "Your name shouldn't have been Randa. It should have been Rahma—Mercy."

"First of all," she replied, "my name isn't Randa. It's Lamis. And second, is there anywhere around here that 'Mercy' could have survived? If I'd been Mercy, I would have died before I was born. I would have died the minute that name flashed into my mother's head. Just look at what's happening: they're killing everything. And you know why? Because they killed mercy first."

She picks the impurities out of my dreams the way we pick little pebbles and clods of dirt out of lentils and cracked wheat before we cook them. I used to look at her fingers and think: if they weren't so delicate, she wouldn't be able to do that.

But she does it perfectly. If she sits next to me while I'm sleeping, I don't have any nightmares. As if she'd spread a net to keep out the things that shouldn't get in, she keeps me from dreaming about things that would scare me awake.

One time I asked her how she did that.

"Do what?" she said.

"Come on now, Randa. You know and I know."

"I swear I don't know what you're talking about!"

I didn't want to say it out loud for fear that she might tell me I was crazy. So I didn't. Instead I just said, "I'm better now. Why don't you go sleep in your own bed? Don't you miss it?"

All she could say was, "And who around here would sleep at all when he knows he might never wake up?"

You see? The things she says come from some deep place.

Another time she said to me, "When they close the roads and hem us in from the sky, I go roaming inside myself. I have to, Auntie. When I do that, I come across things I didn't know existed. And you know what they are? Words. They take me by the hand and lead me along. They glow, and when they come together, a big sun rises, and I see more. I feel more. I see you, even. I see Lamis, Saleh, Jamal, my brothers. I see Grandma. I see all of you. And I understand you better."

But she didn't tell me what she saw on the television screen that day as we sat there looking at it but not watching it. She didn't say. It was only later that she told me she'd known, but had wanted me to find out for myself. She said, "There are things you need to find out on your own. If somebody else tells you, they don't mean anything."

Even though she didn't tell me that day, I sensed what had happened. I just didn't want to know. I didn't want to confirm it.

Without a word, she and I got up and said to Saleh, "You stay here with your sister. We're going on a little errand, and we'll be back."

I didn't want to get agitated or cry, since I knew that if I did, I'd be giving away the fact that you'd died. I wanted you to come to me. I wanted you to send me those short signals of yours that used to tell me where I could find you.

But Saleh refused to stay home. So we called Lamis to come. I asked her if she could babysit Nadia while we went on an errand.

Randa wasn't saying a word. She kept so quiet, you would have thought she didn't know how to talk. When Lamis got there, I figured Saleh would change his mind and stay home. But he didn't.

That's when I got scared. I thought to myself: he knows what's happened, and so does Randa. I'm the only one who's in denial.

The person on the TV screen had been bloodied beyond recognition. In fact, I wondered if I'd seen a face at all. For all I knew, by some bizarre coincidence severed body parts had come together in the shape of a face that wasn't necessarily yours.

I thought back on how, every time I saw you, you'd looked different from the time before. It dismayed me at first. I thought: what is this occupation doing to me? It keeps throwing me into the arms of somebody I've never seen before.

Now, don't misunderstand me here: you know how much I love you. But it still scared me.

I remember that time when I didn't know who you were, and I said, "Shame on you! What's an old man like you doing running after a girl half his age!" Then you started to laugh your head off, and if you hadn't, I never would have recognized you!

Another time when you were following me, I thought you were a spy. You'd been trailing me from the time I left the house. It had never occurred to me that you might come that close to home, and I was always super cautious. I'd been trying to get you off my trail, but I finally gave up and headed back to our neighborhood. When you kept after me, I screamed, "Spy! Spy!" So the boys started chasing you away with rocks. But thankfully, you got away from them.

Later you said, "You nearly did me in, Amna! You've got to be careful, of course. But if you take it too far, you could be the death of me."

Even though I knew Gaza was crawling with spies, I stopped screaming like that. If I concluded that somebody was a real spy, I was prepared to go running around all day just to wear him out. I also developed more patience, so that I was all right with the idea of coming home sometimes without getting to see you.

According to the TV newscast, the plane that had dropped the rocket had left one dead and another critically wounded.

Then they showed a picture of the victim and asked those who knew him to come to al-Shifa Hospital right away.

Randa's silence scared me. But when she realized that Saleh would be coming with us, she finally opened her mouth.

"Hopefully everything will be all right."

She said it the way her grandmother might have said it—like somebody who knows what's going on but doesn't want to let on.

"Don't worry—it wasn't him," I told her. "If it had been, I would have recognized him right away. Show me his pinky, and I could tell you if it's him or not."

I knew those scattered body parts couldn't possibly be you. I mean: where was your height? Where were your eyes? Your hands? Your smile? Your step? No, it couldn't have been you.

But then everything changed. When we got to the hospital, it was pandemonium. Hundreds of people had come to identify you, and everybody was crying.

When we finally managed to make our way through the crowd, we came up to a man wearing a blood-spattered white coat at the entrance to the morgue.

"I want to see him," I told him.

"Are you a relative of his?" he asked.

"He's my husband."

"Twenty women have come up saying he's they're husband!"

"Twenty? Jamal only had one wife, and that was me."

"That's what they're all saying. Anyway, go ahead."

When Saleh started to go in, the man stopped him. "You're the only one allowed in," he said to me. So Saleh stayed outside with Randa.

He uncovered you, but I couldn't see a thing. Even the parts of the body that hadn't been completely charred by the blast had been blackened by the smoke. I searched for something that would indicate it was you, but I couldn't find anything. I asked him to pull the sheet back a little more.

"There's nothing left to see, Ma'am," he said. But he pulled it back anyway. I started to cry. Then I started screaming, "Jamal! Jamal!"

"Do you recognize him?" he asked.

But I couldn't speak. All I could do was scream, louder and louder.

A nurse came up, put her arm around me, and led me toward the outer entrance. The minute I caught a glimpse of Saleh, my tears dried up and my screaming stopped as if nothing had happened.

I saw you. I saw you in his face.

When Randa asked me about it, I said, "No, it wasn't him."

When Saleh asked me, I said, "It wasn't him."

And when I asked myself, I said the same thing.

"Okay, then," Randa said, "let's go home."

"No," I told her, clinging to the darkness of the night.

She understood me.

"I'll go and come back, then," she said.

Taking Saleh by the hand, she led him away. He followed her so calmly, it was as though she were his mother, not me, which scared me even more.

I sat down at the hospital entrance. After a while I realized that I was sitting back to back with another woman.

When I asked her who she was, she said, "I'm his wife."

"But *I'm* his wife." I objected.

Another woman heard us and chimed in, "I know the one you're talking about, and *I'm* his wife!"

Still another woman claimed she was his mother. And nobody, she declared, can know these things the way a mother does.

We got quiet, and stayed that way for a long time. Then another woman said, "I'm sure he's my husband."

"He's all I've got," a teenage girl declared. "He's my only brother. Why do you want to take him away from me?"

More silence.

Then I heard a little boy screaming, "Baba, Baba! I want my baba!"

I shot to my feet.

"Where are you going?" asked one of the women who'd told me you were her husband. She was sure of it, too. She said she'd had seven children by you—three daughters and four sons. When I heard her talking that way, I thought to myself: well, a woman who's had that many kids by somebody must know him better than I'd know somebody I've had only two kids by.

"Where are you going?" she asked again. It was as if she didn't want me to leave—as if she wanted me to be his wife instead of her.

"Didn't they say on the television that somebody had been wounded?" I asked her.

"That's what they said," she affirmed. "They say he's in a coma he might never come out of. Half his head was blown off."

I sat back down.

No fewer than ten wakes were held: in Jabaliya, al-Shati, al-Nusayrat, al-Breij, al-Maghazi, Deir al-Balah, and Khan Yunis. Some of the people who came to offer their condolences told me they'd been to wakes in Rafah, too.

Even when they saw their brothers Jawad and Salim at the funeral-turned-demonstration, Randa and Lamis didn't find out whether it had been you or not. "Time will tell," was all they had to say.

But it turned out not to be that simple.

Afraid to leave

"LET HIM SLEEP," I TOLD Amna. "Let him sleep!"

I've seen a lot in Gaza, and I've heard about plenty more on the West Bank. But what happened here in the Martyrs' Cemetery was something I'd never seen before.

A bunch of women had circled the grave and were crying over whoever was buried there. Every single one of them was convinced that the person in the grave was her husband, her son, her brother, or her sweetheart, and every one of them had her eye on the cemetery entrance, hoping against hope that her beloved would show up all of a sudden and say, "And what are *you* doing here?"

There was nothing to indicate that the person buried there was him. Nothing, that is, but that vague sort of feeling that closes in on your heart from all sides until there's nothing left of it but a mass of sorrow.

"Let him sleep," I told her.

"But I'm afraid that if I leave, some other woman will come along and take him away from me."

*

The other women who'd gathered at the grave looked just as sad as Amna did, and just as afraid of losing the person lying there. They seemed to have tacitly agreed to divide these feelings among themselves so that in a few days' time, the vague possessiveness each of them harbored might give way to a sense that the person they were mourning—or afraid to lose—belonged as much to each one of them as he did to all the others.

There were boys who would come and cry for a while—some less, some more. A few days later you might see them playing together among the graves, like brothers who'd realized that the person buried there was a father to all of them. It was as if they'd reached the same conclusion the women had when, as they talked about Gaza's young men near and far, they referred to them all as "our boys."

As the days passed, I began hearing different stories about this person to whom their sorrows clung. According to one, he'd been wanted by the occupation authorities. According to others, he'd died one day on his way home, or on his way to a demonstration, or a funeral, or some unknown destination.

One woman wailed, "We'd only been married for six months! How could they murder him just like that? He didn't even get to see his son!" As she spoke, she held her unborn child close as though he were in her arms.

Another said, "He was my fiancé!" Grieved over his loss and the loss of the chance to wear the white wedding dress she'd dreamed of, she went on and on about how wonderful he'd been.

A third woman reminisced, "He used to say, 'There's death all around us. But we're still here, and we'll live to see our grandchildren.' He was excited about becoming a grandfather. When we got married, he was in his early twenties, and I was nineteen. 'Hopefully we'll be liberated from the occupation,' I told him, 'and you'll see your great-children, too.' But all he said was, 'People are dying off faster and faster now.' He knew he wasn't going to see his grandson. It breaks your heart to be just steps away from somebody you're hoping to see, only to have them put your eyes out like that."

A fourth said, "He was all I had here. My family's scattered all over—everybody's in a different country."

When evening came, either the mothers would round up their children, or the children would come on their own to take their mothers home. The girl who'd lost her fiancé would gather her black skirts in preparation to leave, and a couple of girls who always came and left together would slip quietly away. All I knew was that the deceased had been like a brother, a father, a son, and a fiancé to them. "And more," one of them added.

Out of respect for their grief, the other women held back from asking them too many questions.

In the end, the only one left was Amna, the unofficial keeper of the grave.

In the mornings, the other women would bring her food, but she never touched it, and most days the children ended up gobbling it down.

Then all of a sudden the bereaved fiancée stopped coming. She was gone for three days. One of the women said, "We've got to go ask about her. Maybe something's happened to her." But on the fourth day she came back.

"What happened?" we asked her after she'd sat down. She didn't say anything. Then she burst into tears. She cried so hard and so long, we concluded that she must have confirmed that the person in the grave really was her fiancé, after all.

"Did the man in the coma wake up and talk?" one of the women asked her.

"No."

"Why are you crying, then?"

"Well," she said, hesitating, "I don't know what to say to you all, I'm so ashamed of myself. Yesterday he came back!"

A deep silence followed.

None of them knew whether to rejoice for this young woman over the return of her fiancé, or to cry for herself because the chances of the person in the grave being her own loved one were that much greater now.

Finally, the woman who was about to become a grandmother said to her, "My fiancé and I married and had a family and we got to enjoy our children. You have every right to do the same. Congratulations!"

This just made the girl cry harder.

"How can I go off and leave you here all by yourselves?"

"You can do it because you have to. Now go!"

"If I knew who this martyr was, I'd name my son after him. But there are all sorts of names in that grave."

"Go get married and have a family. Names are the least of our worries now. Look at us: every one of us has her own name for the person buried here. What matters isn't the name, but the human being who died."

As sunset approached, the girl made sure she wasn't the first to leave the graveside. She stayed put until there were so many children shouting and wailing that their mothers had no choice but to take them home. When she did get up at last, she said, "I'll be back."

"No!" they cried out in a chorus. "Don't you dare!"

Every now and then the girl would bring a pot of tea and some food, and then sit down without saying a word. A number of the women tried to encourage her not to be so sad over her good fortune.

She'd cry—sometimes a lot, sometimes a little. And then she'd disappear.

Within a couple of weeks, only five women were still coming every day.

"There are only five of us left," one remarked.

"But there's only person in the grave," remarked another.

"I think there are only four of us, actually," another broke in. "There's a lady whose house was shelled in al-Maghazi, and she was killed."

"Who?"

"Umm Fuad."

Suddenly they forgot all about the person in the grave and started crying over their companion in grief.

"She died before she could find out whether the person buried here was her husband or not."

"She'll find out before we do."

Amna's tears seemed to stream out in all directions as if she were crying for a million different people at once.

"You've got to go back to Nadia and Saleh," I told her.

"What? Are you tired of them?" she asked.

Saleh and two-year-old Nadia had been part of our family from the night we went to the hospital. The person we worried about most, actually, was my mom. Whenever she fed Nadia or changed her diaper, she would start weeping uncontrollably.

"But why cry now?" I probed. "Do you want us to make Saleh feel even worse?"

She dried her eyes with the hem of her sleeve.

After a while she got so she could hold back her tears during the day. But as soon as Nadia and Saleh had gone to sleep, she would sob nonstop.

When I asked her, "Why are you crying now?" she'd say, "Who are you—Lamis or Randa?"

"Actually, I don't know, Mama!"

"Anyway, whichever one you are—you ask me why I'm crying? If I don't cry now, when will I cry? Why isn't everybody in Gaza crying their eyes out right now? Why are we supposed to trill with joy all the time? We're expected to do that because our kids are martyrs, and that's an honor. But they're *our kids*. Every day, every hour, every minute I expect somebody to knock on my door and bring me news I don't want to hear. We worry and we worry and we worry. And in the end I'm expected to trill like somebody who's got something to be happy about! Do you know why mothers are constantly crying over their kids? It's so that, if they lose them, they won't have to feel so ashamed over that trill they have to let out because the world demands it of them. A mother cries all day long because she knows the time is coming when she'll be forced to betray her sorrows by trilling as though she were the happiest woman alive. But do you know who it is that makes us do that? It isn't our families and neighbors. No, the ones who force us to trill at the funerals of the people we love are the ones who murdered them. We do it so as not to let them feel, even for a moment, that they've defeated us. But if we live to see this occupation end, we're going to cry and cry! We're going to cry over all the people whose funerals we had to trill at. We're going to be sad when we want to, and happy when we want to—not at the times set by the people who're shooting at us. We're not really heroes, you know. We just have to act as if we were."

That day I got really worried about my mom and my two brothers.

In the morning Amna picked Nadia up and took Saleh by the hand, and we went to the cemetery. As we approached, I saw the women from a distance. The more their number shrank, the more worried I got. At first they'd been able to spread their sadness around, since there had been more of them to share in it. But every time one of them disappeared, she'd leave her share of grief on the others' hearts.

Amna held Nadia close, but she wasn't crying. Something inside her made her hold herself together when Saleh was around.

"I told you it was him," she said.

"Don't give up hope," my mother urged her.

"I'll go to the hospital and ask," I volunteered.

As I read the date of death on the temporary gravestone, I wondered: what name will end up here? Does a date go looking for a name to fill the scary blank space above it? Or does a name go looking for a date to give it more meaning and effect? Maybe each of them goes looking for the other. If so, which of them suffers more in the search?

"I'll go to the hospital today," I said again.

"No," she pleaded, "don't do that! If he didn't die in the rocket attack, then he died from being away from me for so long. Either way, it has to be him."

I went anyway, but I didn't dare come back with that name, with that whole name.

Before I opened my mouth, she said, "You should have believed me before. Anyway, do you believe me now?"

I nodded.

The two girls were the last ones to leave Amna. They stood up and hugged her without a word.

Is there anything left to say? I thought to myself as they walked away.

Even so, something inside me prompted me to get up and run after them. I caught up with them at the cemetery entrance. When they heard my footsteps behind them, they stopped and waited.

"We've lived by ourselves for a long time," they said. "So we know what it's like not to have anybody."

I started to ask a question, but before I could get it out, one of them said, "Don't ask."

The other added, "We didn't want to go away before we'd made sure he had somebody. Now things are different. He won't be alone any more."

Then they walked away.

I tried to say something, anything. But I couldn't get a single word to come out.

I sat down and cried.

Angels in disguise

I'M ALONE WITH YOU NOW.

The other women have all gone, and it's just you and me.

Every day or two some of them come back, though, and I know all's well with the world.

I swear, it is.

They come to check on you through me, and on me through you.

"Did you really have to burn those pictures?" Saleh yelled. "We could have had something to remember him by!" Then he burst into tears.

I hadn't wanted the pictures to make him sad.

"You know they bombed the cemetery?" I asked him. "Why would they bomb a cemetery? It's because they never get tired of looking for pictures of the people they've murdered. Randa tells me they wanted to make sure the people they'd killed were really dead."

Then, relenting, I said, "Okay. I'll give you one."

"I want them all."

Now how did that boy know all the pictures were still around, hidden away somewhere?

Maybe I'd been even more afraid than he was—afraid a time would come when all I had left of you was memories. Memories that I love and hate, that come and go without leaving us anything but madness. Memories that have gotten so old that they stop helping us conjure a single face we love and need.

All those other women have left.

The person lying here might not have turned out to be you, but one of their loved ones. You might have turned up alive somewhere.

It feels awful to want you for myself, and to want you for all of them, too.

But the worst thing would be for you to be mine, and then to become somebody else's. I'm not an angel.

Umm Fuad, the lady who was martyred recently—you know her, right? There were times when I thought the person buried here was hers. And when she was killed, I concluded that you really did belong to her. I felt that the person lying in this grave deserved something big. He deserved to have somebody join him, and that's what she did. She joined him as a fellow martyr. I concluded that God must love her more than the rest of us, and I wondered what we'd done to deserve all this suffering. We all felt as though she'd taken you away, and there were moments when I thought the grave we were sitting around was empty. As for the children, they were too young to be conscious of something they couldn't see. Except for Saleh, who went completely silent. Nothing mattered to him any more—not even Lamis.

So one day I told Lamis, "Take him to the sea! Maybe he'll drown his sorrows there and open up to you."

But he wouldn't go.

As for little Nadia, she was blissfully ignorant of what was going on around her. She could even laugh.

A few days ago she broke loose from Umm Jawad's hand and went running around the cemetery. Little kids have no idea what kind of a place it is.

When she laughed like that, I felt mortified, as if it had been me laughing. After all, isn't she a little piece of me? She came out of my body and before I knew it, she was walking around. A little miracle. Imagine: you watch as a part of your body gets bigger and bigger and bigger. Then all of a sudden it separates from you and starts to cry. Then it starts to laugh. Then it starts running away from you. At first you catch up with it. But after a while it finds its wings and flies away. We end up being scattered here and there through our children. You know why? Because when Death comes, we want to make sure part of us escaped from it.

But it ends up catching up with them, too, you say?

You're right, it does. But by that time, hopefully they're scattered here and there through *their* children as well.

You're not the only one who's on the run. All of us here are. All of us.

Take Nadia, for example. She doesn't know it, but she's racing toward the day when she'll know she lost you. As she moves forward, she'll discover that she's actually moving backward, toward you. She's approaching the big, heavy question she's bound to ask me one of these nights: "Where is he?"

And when it comes, I'll look for an answer that's bearable for both my heart and hers.

Like I said: it's just you and me now.

Has the situation gotten any better—in your body, I mean? Did they give you back its missing parts? We're born whole. So why do we have to die this way?

Umm Jawad says to me, "You've got to go home to your children now."

And Randa's told me the same thing. When she came to write your name over the date on the tombstone, she talked about how unfair history is. It's unfair, she said, because a hundred years of sacrifices still haven't convinced it that we know more about life than people who make an art of pulling it up by the roots. She said it was like an unquenchable fire. We scream in its face, "So you want more? Here!" And we cry. "You want more? Take these, then! You aren't satisfied with the ones that died in scattered incidents today? You want a massacre? Then here!" And we cry some more. And all the while, we're living for that moment when it tells us all of a sudden, "I've had enough."

I'll be back. I know I have to go, of course, because you're telling me so. But that's the only reason I have to.

I'll be back. I didn't know I'd live to see two pieces of my heart in a single graveyard.

When Mustafa was martyred, you said, "Don't be afraid. I'm with you." That strengthened me a little even though Mustafa wasn't with me any more and wouldn't be coming back. Some settlers shot him to death because the car he was in was trying to pass theirs. Can you imagine that? Is that a reason for somebody to die around here?

I once said to you, "If that was bound to happen to him, then it's just as well that it happened when it did, before Saleh and Nadia were old enough to know him. If they had gotten to know him, it would have been a catastrophe. I mean, how could they have borne to part with somebody like him? And what makes it even worse is that he was gone in a split second—just like that—and for no reason!

I'll be back. Don't worry about us.

We'll stay in your sight. In front of you. Around you.

You know, from the very start I had a sinking feeling that my life with you would be short, even if we had a hundred years together. So I knew it would be short to begin with, and then they came along with their tanks and their airplanes and their generals to cut it even shorter. It's as if every year they subtract from our lives is added to theirs. At this rate, they'll end up immortal.

In any case, I'll be back.

I won't go away.

Yesterday I was talking to Randa (who's stopped telling me she's Lamis, by the way), and I asked her about those two girls who kept coming to your grave.

I said, "Remember how sad they were all the time? But they didn't talk much, did they? They seemed to be keeping some sort of big secret. I was almost afraid you'd been married to one of them! Otherwise, where would you have slept during all that time after you disappeared? I was going to ask them, and I had a feeling some of the other women wanted to, too. But none of us did. And you know why? Because at some point we discovered that we all loved you, and that maybe you didn't belong to any one of us completely. But after it turned out that you were you, I asked Randa what she knew, and she said, "You're not going to believe what I have to tell you.""

I swore to her that I would believe her.

"You're still not going to believe it."

"Yes, I will," I insisted.

You want to know too now, don't you? I mean, who could help feeling curious if he saw two stunning young women running their hands that lovingly over somebody's grave?

Anyway, Randa said, "So you promise you'll believe me, then?"

"I promise," I said. "Now for God's sake, don't keep me in suspense any longer. I can't stand it!"

Then, with a matter-of-factness that unsettled me, she said, "They're angels."

"No!" I blurted out. "That's impossible."

"See! I told you you wouldn't believe me."

Well, anyway, that evening I saw them come back, and for the first time I saw their wings. They were more beautiful than before. A lot more beautiful. They gave off a kind of translucent glow. They kept coming closer and closer until they were right next to me. Then all of a sudden I heard them speak, and it was like nothing I'd ever heard before. Their voices sounded as if they were made of light. Then they lowered their wings over me and said, "Go now. Don't worry about him. He won't be lonely with us. We'll stay here till you get back."

And that's the way it's been ever since: as soon as I get to the cemetery entrance, I see them there by your grave. They slip away so gently, they wouldn't even scratch the air. They wave and leave the cemetery from the other side.

In any case, yesterday I said to Randa, "I know I've lost my marbles, but don't laugh at me. Now, what I'm thinking is this: nobody's ever been able to prove that angels can be either male or female. So how did *you* manage to do that?"

Then she told me her story from beginning to end, and for the first time I realized that people really can be angels.

"Now I believe you," I told her.

Who would have thought?

THE PICTURES OF JAMAL THAT Amna had hidden away, and which she placed in her son's hands one morning, sparked new life in the boy. They transformed him into a new person, one we'd never known before, and would never have imagined.

He cinched his belt, combed his hair, and asked his mother, "Do I really look like him?" After repeating the question a second time, he picked up the photos as though he were going on a mission.

"Yes," she said. "You look a lot like him."

"What do I need to do to look exactly like him?"

"You just need to grow up a little more."

"Is that all? I think his hair was longer than mine, so I need to grow it out. From now on I've got to look just like him."

"Take care of yourself," Amna told him with a nod.

He came and knocked on our window-turned-door.

Lamis answered. Flustered, he took a couple of steps back. I invited him in, and he made an awkward entrance.

Even under the most ordinary circumstances, Lamis's presence would have been enough to reduce him to a pool of sweat. How much more, then, now that he was all dressed up with his neatly combed hair, his trousers all belted up, and his bright, shiny face?

"I'll leave the two of you alone," Lamis announced, and exited the room.

I watched him follow her out with his eyes, on the verge of tears.

"Well, aren't *you* looking chic, Mr. Saleh!" I said brightly.

"Lower your voice," he whispered.

"Well, aren't *you* looking chic, Mr. Saleh!" I said again, this time in a barely audible whisper.

"Do I look like him?" he asked.

"Like who?"

"My dad."

I moved my head back slightly and took another look at him. His features tensed up as though he were waiting for a verdict that would seal his eternal destiny.

"Actually," I said, "you do."

"How much?"

"A lot."

"My mom told me the same thing. But how can I look exactly like him?"

"That's simple."

"What do you mean, simple? Tell me!"

"You just need to grow up a little more."

"What's going on around here? My mom says something, and then you say the very same thing."

"So is that what your mom told you?"

"Word for word!"

"Well, then, you should believe us."

"But I want to look like him right now!"

Every now and then he would glance over at the door that led out to the courtyard between our houses, either fearfully, or in hopes that Lamis would appear.

"Where did she go?"

"Lamis?"

He nodded.

"She must be with my grandma, or helping our mom. Shall I call her?"

"No."

"Why are you asking about her?"

"I don't know."

"But I know."

"You know why?"

"She means a lot to you, doesn't she?"

"Yeah."

"I mean, a whole lot. Right?"

"Right."

"A *whole, whole* lot. Right?"

"Have you seen all his pictures?"

"Whose pictures?"

"My dad's."

Since his question was less of a question than a way of escaping my interrogation, there was no need to answer it. He knew I knew, and that made him uncomfortable, especially when Lamis came into the room. Suddenly all eyes were on him as if he were the one who'd just walked in and not her.

A few days earlier she'd moaned to me, "Our whole life's ruined! Things are so bad, I feel like going out in the street and giving Saleh what he wants just so he can tell me out loud, 'I love you, Lamis!' Only I know he wouldn't. What am I thinking, anyway? Do I want a boy half my age to stand in the street like a cucumber vendor shouting, 'I love you, Lamis!'? You know, Randa? It was really sort of nice when he did that before. It was cute. I admit, it used to make me mad sometimes, but now I see how sweet it was. It might be the nicest thing I can remember ever happening in our neighborhood. It wasn't even that long ago, but he's not a little boy any more. We're not what we used to be. We're not even ourselves completely. I feel as though the things we do and say, and the things that scare us, or make us happy and sad, don't reflect who we really are."

"Would you mind if I wrote down what you just said?" I asked.

"Go ahead. Words like these may be the only thing left in the end, I suppose."

So I wrote what she'd said in my notebook. I also wrote, "Freedom is the only thing that brings you into harmony with yourself. Without freedom, nothing's in harmony with

126

itself—not the streets, or the sea, or the sky, or the morning, or Grandma's coffee, or the flowers, or love, or life, or childhood, or old age. Even the cemetery can't be itself around here, because it isn't free to grow at a natural pace. It's born and gets old the way the occupiers want it to, not the way it wants to."

"Will they bury him here?"

"No, over there."

"There? Why?"

"Because the cemetery's full."

"Full? How's that?"

"Because there's so much death. There's just so much death."

"Love him a little," I said to Lamis.

"If it matters that much to you, then love him yourself! What's there for me to love about him when he's so young?"

"In a few more years he'll be a guy, and the age difference we see now won't be there any more. Then you won't feel you're so much older than he is."

"He's a boy."

"He's a little bigger than that."

I looked around. Saleh had disappeared.

I went out in the yard and opened the iron gate that leads onto the street. I looked both ways. I saw him knocking on our neighbors' door.

The neighbor lady came out, and I heard him asking her a question: "Have you seen the pictures of my dad?"

"No," she replied.

"I'll show them to you, then."

"All right. Come on in."

"No thanks. I've got a lot of work to do."

So he did his photo presentation while she stood at the door. After going through them one by one, he said, "Does he look like me?"

"Yes, quite a bit."

"Why doesn't anybody tell me he looks *just* like me?" he blurted out.

As the neighbor lady stood there perplexed, not knowing what to say, I saw him head toward the next house. He knocked again.

Everybody in the whole neighborhood saw Jamal's pictures that day. Saleh carried them from house to house, holding onto them with the greatest of care and being careful not to let anyone else touch them. If he saw anyone reaching out for them, he'd pull them back quickly, saying, "No touching!"

After making his rounds, he came back crestfallen.

"Nobody tells me I look just like him!" he grumbled. "They all say, 'You look a lot like him.' So, do you think I should ask Lamis, too?"

"Lamis?" His question took me by surprise. "I wish you would!"

"Why do you say, 'I wish you would'?" he wanted to know.

"No reason," I said awkwardly. "I just think Lamis is the person you should have asked from the start."

"You mean it's too late to ask her now?"

"No, not at all. There's no such thing as 'too late' when it comes to things like this. All that matters is for it to happen in the end, for you to ask her."

"Lamis! Lamis!"

"No! Don't call her now!"

"When should I call her, then? Lamis!"

Lamis stuck her head around the door as though she'd been standing behind it the entire time. I'd forgotten that our houses were only a couple of meters apart.

"What's up?"

"Saleh wants to ask you a question."

"Ask away."

I got up to leave. As I passed her, I poked her as if to say, "Be nice to him, will you?"

"Stay here," he said to me.

"I'm just going to the bathroom," I fibbed. "I'll be right back."

I left the room and parked myself a couple of steps away from the door.

It got so quiet that if I hadn't just left the room knowing there were a couple of people inside, I would have thought it was empty.

"How are you, Saleh?"

"Good. But not that good."

Things got quiet again.

"You wanted to say something to me?"

"Right."

"What is it?"

"I wanted to ask you a question."

"Go ahead."

"Before I ask, I have to show you the pictures of my dad. Now, do you promise to tell me the truth?"

"I swear."

"What do you swear?"

"To tell the truth."

"Okay, then. Now things are clear. You know, boys always play tricks on you by swearing to something without telling you what it was, and you find out later that it wasn't what you thought!"

"Don't worry."

More silence. I could almost hear the photos sliding against each other. Then I heard him say, "You can hold them yourself if you'd like."

My jaw nearly dropped to the floor.

Had I heard him right? Had he actually given somebody permission to touch his precious pictures?

"So he really does look like me? Really, really? You did swear, remember!"

"No, really. He looks just like you."

Suddenly I heard the boy whoop as if he were watching a football game and his team had just scored a winning goal.

"Now I know why I love you so much!"

When I walked back in the room, I found Lamis alone, a somber look on her face.

"Where did he disappear to?" I asked.

She pointed to the door that led to their yard.

If I were blind

IF I WERE BLIND, I'D say there's more death around here than there is life.

But every time I'm about to reach this conclusion, I open the door, lean against the doorframe, and watch the kids in the street.

There are always new bunches of them, and all the same age. They seem to appear out of nowhere, like almond or lemon blossoms. Whole groups of them that I've never even seen before. They come racing down the street, tripping and falling and getting up again, and by the time they know how to make it to the corner on their own, a new flock has shown up. The new one fills the street and pushes the old one out into the wider world as mothers peek out at them anxiously through half-opened windows and doors.

If I were blind, I'd say there's more death around here than there is life. Death swoops down, ripping the life cycle to shreds before it's finished. It's no wonder families worry about their children whenever they hear gunshots, and whenever darkness falls.

All of a sudden children are born, grow up, leave the neighborhood, and die. What might they have become if they had survived?

A few days ago I read the transcript of an interview with an Israeli sniper who admitted that his commanding officers had asked him not to shoot any child under the age of twelve.

The journalist asked him, "When you're sitting behind a barrier or in a tower, how can you tell whether a child is above or below this age?"

"Well," the sniper replied, "we can't tell a kid to pull out his birth certificate before we kill him."

Saleh picked up the photos and headed for the spot where his dad had been martyred. He didn't know the way, but he kept asking people for directions until he found it. Once there, he stood for hours on top of the ashes that remained from the explosion, and whenever anybody passed by he would stop him and say, "Do you recognize this man? He's my dad. This is where he was martyred."

Meanwhile, we had no idea where he'd gone. We looked all over for him. We asked in hospitals, in national security centers, in one neighborhood after another, but there was no sign of him.

We were all crying, afraid Amna would get back before he did.

My sister said, "There's only one place left to look."

"Where's that?" we asked.

"The place where his dad was killed. He asked me about it."

So off we went. And that's where we found him. When I came up to him, he looked at me as if he'd never seen me before.

"Do you recognize this man? He's my dad, and this is where he was martyred."

"I know," I said.

He was so exhausted, his legs could hardly hold him up any more.

We brought him to our house, and by the time Amna got back, he was asleep.

She wanted to wake him up and have him sleep in his own bed.

"Leave him here till morning," we said. "The boy's worn out."

"But how can I sleep there alone with Nadia?"

"You could sleep here," my mom suggested.

Grandma was watching the scene with tears in her eyes. "But . . . ."

"Now don't you 'but' me," said my mom. "Think of all the times we've slept at your house."

After that it wasn't hard to track him down when he disappeared, although we made a point of not letting him disappear in the first place.

One day he said to me, "I can't sleep any more."

That night, we woke to the sound of Amna screaming.

We went running to her house. Her pained cry jolted even Grandma awake. When we got there, she was pointing to Saleh's empty bed. She couldn't talk. All she could do was scream.

The three of us—Amna, my mom, and I—went running through the streets.

We told Lamis to stay at the house. After Samer was martyred, we'd started worrying more about her. And we'd gone on worrying even though it had been years since his death. Something made her seem like the baby of the family despite the fact that she and I had been born only five minutes apart. What worried us most was that she never talked about Samer. It was as if he'd never waved to her from the street corner just steps away from our house. As if he'd never existed.

We combed every street in the camp, but couldn't find him anywhere. It finally occurred to us that maybe he'd gone home, and sure enough, when we got back he was asleep in his bed.

Amna wanted to wake him up. My mom took her by the hand. She was trembling.

"Leave him be. He doesn't sleep well any more. Just be thankful he was finally able to."

When I think back on Lamis and Saleh now, I can see that they had more of a connection than they seemed to on the surface. It wasn't just my fear that the two of them would disappear all of a sudden. It was a deep something-or-other that I can't quite put my finger on.

Saleh said to me, "I've promised myself not to give the occupiers any rest at night. After all, I can't sleep. So why should I let them?" He also told me Lamis had promised him not to give them any rest during the day.

"So," I remarked, "you finally agree on something."

"We've never disagreed."

When I asked him to explain, he said, "All I know is that that's what she told me."

After Samer was martyred, Lamis went to her room and turned the mirror around to face the wall. When I went in, I found her looking at the back of the mirror as though she could see her reflection.

When Samer died, Lamis seemed to change overnight. For one thing, she seemed all of a sudden to have discovered the existence of pop songs. She listened to them nonstop, and made constant shuttles between the front gate and the mirror like a train rushing breathlessly back and forth between two stations.

"That girl's about to go crazy," Grandma said to me.

"Why do you say that?"

"Don't you see her? She stands in front of the mirror all day long!"

"I don't understand."

"Well," she said, "the quickest way to drive yourself crazy is to stand for a long time in front of a mirror."

"Why's that?"

"Because when you do that, you see your reflection more than you see yourself."

"And what does that mean?"

"It means you recognize yourself in the mirror better than you recognize yourself outside of it. In other words, you see yourself as a fantasy more than as a reality. Then after a while, all you see is the copy, and the original disappears."

"You're scaring me, Grandma."

"No, don't be scared. You sister's still safe. As soon as she realizes that stinker is going to see her, and that he dreams about her, her reflection will come out of the mirror, because she'll see *him* in it. And then she'll come back to reality."

"I swear, I don't know what you're talking about, Grandma!"

"You're still young. It's too early for you to understand things like this."

"What do you mean, it's too early for me to understand, Grandma? Okay, so I've got a puny head. But I swear to God, I understand everything."

"You still aren't getting my point."

"Let me write it down, then. Then maybe I'll figure it out some day. Can you repeat what you said?"

"For heaven's sake! How do you expect me to repeat something as important as what I just said? You can't repeat something like that! It only comes out that way once, and that's that."

"Please, Grandma—for my sake!"

"Okay, I'll try. I can repeat the gist of it, at least."

I went and got my notebook. She repeated what she'd said as I scribbled. When we'd finished, she said, "And what are you going to do with what your grandma said? I'm afraid I might see it in the newspapers after you grow up."

"Don't worry."

"What I said was for your ears alone, Randa. After I'm gone, I don't want people saying, 'Wasfiya said this, and she didn't say that.'"

Looking at me intently, she added, "I've told you these things because you're going to understand. I know you've got a little head. But there's a good brain inside it."

Saleh seemed to be the only person who reminded Lamis of Samer. We'd close our eyes and see him closer to her than anybody else. But the second we opened them again, we'd see her pushing him away, as if he were the cause of everything that had happened. Then his closeness to her would seem like a miracle that had taken place once upon a dream that bore no connection to reality.

This used to confuse him really badly, and more than once he cried.

"But Lamis isn't like that!" he insisted.

I asked him to explain. And when he did, I could hardly believe my ears.

She was always trying to make us think she would never forgive him. But when we weren't around, she would do just the opposite.

I started keeping my eye on the mirror. I even went so far as to put a string on it so that I could tell whether she had turned it around to see herself when we weren't looking. But she never turned it around once, and that scared me.

When I told Grandma about it, she said, "The girl slipped out of our hands while we were looking right at her."

If I call her, she'll answer

"I'M THE ONLY ONE WHO knows where she is, and if I call her, she'll answer."

"For God's sake, Saleh!" I said, "You and your sister are all I've got. Lamis will come back on her own. She's old enough not to lose her way home."

"But Baba was older than Lamis, and he didn't make it back."

When Randa started to cry, he said to her, "Give me her picture."

"Later," she said. "I'll give it to you later."

Then he stole the mirror when nobody was looking!

"Fortunately," he told me, "the mirror was facing the wall the whole time."

Before I could ask him how he knew this, he said, "Because Lamis's image had stayed in it."

"I know how hard life can get, Saleh," I told him. "But as long as we're together, we can make it. I know how sometimes we feel like the world's closing in on us from all sides, and we have to get some air. But I'd asked you not to leave the house without telling me."

One time he said to me, "If there were nobody in the world but Lamis . . . and you . . . and Nadia and Baba . . . and we were here all alone without any soldiers, the sky and the sea would be more beautiful."

When I told Randa what he'd said, it made her happy. At the same time, she admitted she was worried about him, and she asked me if she could write down what he'd said.

"Why not?" I said.

So she went and got her notebook, and started writing and writing.

"You're writing more than what he said," I observed.

"Don't worry," she said. "I'm also writing down when he said it, and who he said it to."

When I first got to know Randa, she was collecting pictures of martyred children. She cried because she had so many. Then she got the saddest look on her face. It was the saddest look I'd ever seen in my life.

"What's wrong, Randa?" I asked.

"Some of these people had never had their pictures taken before. The only picture we have of them is the one that was taken after they were already dead."

She started to cry over the fact that some of the pictures didn't even look like the people they'd been taken of. They'd been so disfigured by the bullets and the shrapnel—by Death—you wouldn't have recognized them.

"How can I put pictures like these along with the others when I know they were so much more beautiful before?"

"You could write about them," I suggested. "Write down some of the things they'd said, the things they'd dreamed of."

From that day on, she wouldn't let her mother go to a single wake without her. As the women cried and talked, she would sift through their exchanges for the last things these children had done or said. When she got home afterward, she would sit and write. If I came over to see her, her eyes would be red from all the crying she'd been doing.

"Didn't you cry while you were there?" I asked. "Of course I did. It's just that when I write about these kids, I feel as though I know them, as though I'm living through what they lived through, and I realize that while I was at the wake, I didn't cry enough. When I'm sitting here by myself, I feel like they were mine, that I'm the one who lost them."

"God, if only the occupation would end before this notebook runs out."

It looked like ten notebooks stuck together.

She went on, "Sometimes I cry for a reason that might not occur to anybody else, not even to you, Auntie Amna. I cry because my handwriting keeps getting smaller and smaller. I look at how many blank pages are left. Then I go outside and see all the soldiers in the street, and I come back in and cry."

I said to Saleh, "If it weren't for this girl, I would have given up a long time ago. Have you noticed how she speaks to me, and to you, and to Nadia? She never leaves Nadia out. She talks to her as if she were a grown-up. At first this surprised me, but it doesn't any more. Sometimes there are things we don't understand, and we should just let them be."

Lamis wasn't the way she used to be. She'd grown up. But so had Saleh. He'd caught up with her. I mentioned this to Randa, and she wasn't surprised. In fact, she'd said the same thing to Lamis—or something to that effect. Something had changed. There was the fuzz on his upper lip, and the pimples on his nose. But what hadn't changed was his determination to go to the spot where his dad had been martyred. He would stand there and show his dad's pictures to passersby, and they all listened to what he had to say. Some of them cried. They could see he was too young to have this mountain of troubles heaped on his shoulders.

"I want to tell you something, sweet boy. And don't laugh at me the way your dad used to do, or I'll be mad at you both! Anyway, what I want to say is: I was sure Lamis would be your wife."

. . .

"Now there you go laughing! Or are you crying? You're crying. No, I want you to laugh, then. The Gaza Sea has enough saltwater in it already without your tears!"

It made me happy to see that Lamis didn't come running like mad to look for her mirror the way I'd expected her to. She looked at the place where the mirror had been hanging, but she didn't get upset at all.

Randa whispered to me, "Lamis doesn't see herself any more."

"How's that?" I asked.

"Well," she said, "she feels like a ghost, and ghosts don't need mirrors. In fact, a ghost is so delicate, its image might wound it."

On the rare days when you couldn't hear any shooting, when the snipers disappeared and the tanks went searching for God knows what with their gun barrels skyward, Lamis would go up to the roof and look into the distance. Every time she did it, she told us she'd been able to see more than the time before.

Once Randa asked her, "What did you see today?"

All she said was, "It was nothing compared to what I'm going to see tomorrow."

Her answer confused us. So the day after that I asked her myself, and she repeated what she'd said to Randa.

Then Randa started going up to the roof so that she could see what Lamis was seeing.

It was a relief to me that she started to see Saleh more. I thought to myself: maybe she looks into the distance so that she can see him there. But now I wish I hadn't said that. I wish it hadn't even occurred to me.

"So that's how it is!" I said to Randa. "Things had gone this far without my knowing about it? How could you not be honest with me? Why did I have to find out something like this by accident from Lamis, when I was eavesdropping?"

Randa didn't reply. And what could she have said?

But I surprised her. I'd bought the wedding dress, and when she saw it, she was crazy about it. "Please give it to me, Auntie Amna! Please!" she begged.

"No," I told her. "It's for Lamis, and that's that."

"But I *am* Lamis!"

"No, you're not. You're Randa. Don't drive me crazy now!"

"Okay, then, I'm Randa. But haven't you noticed how small the dress is?"

"Of course I have," I retorted. "Do you think I'm blind? And didn't I tell you that people who love each other turn into little birds?"

"You didn't say that about people who love each other. You said it about people who are martyred young."

"Don't you understand me any more, Randa? Why would you say a thing like that? Is there a difference between the first group and the second?"

"I don't know," she murmured.

Imagine that! Randa, the girl who knows everything, admitted there was something she didn't know!

In any case, I said, "Well, if you didn't know before, you do now."

Saleh! Oh, Saleh!

You'll never need another gust of wind!

146

When he was late, she knocked on our door

I CAME OUT AND AMNA said to me, "Saleh is late getting home today, and I have to go to al-Shifa Hospital. There are a lot of children whose families I have to talk to."

She seemed half-dazed.

"When he comes, have him stay at your house till I get back."

Then she left, Nadia's hand in hers.

"And what about Nadia?" I asked her.

"I'll go get her from the nursery myself."

We all knew Saleh had changed after what had happened to his father. He seemed to sense by some sort of filial instinct that his mother wouldn't be able to bear another fatal blow to the heart. (Is there such a thing as a 'filial instinct' along the lines of a 'maternal instinct'? Why shouldn't there be? After all, a son comes out of his mother's womb, doesn't he? He's her flesh and blood, isn't he?)

He stopped leaving the house without asking Amna's permission, and after a while he stopped going anywhere at all. He never let her out of his sight. If he felt she'd taken too long in the other room, he'd get up and go to the room she was in, making up excuses that wouldn't have convinced anybody.

"I'm starting to worry about him," Amna confessed. "I mean, I want him to obey me, but not to this extreme! At first, it seemed the only place he was willing to go was the spot where his dad was martyred. When we told him he'd gone there enough, he stopped going anywhere at all. I want him to get out, to play ball, to . . . and if he wants to throw rocks at some military patrol driving around in the distance, I want him to do that, too!"

Amna would say these things to my mother. Then she would repeat them forlornly to each of us individually. What she didn't realize was that Saleh wasn't acting this way in order to please or obey her. He was doing it because he was worried about her. Rather than not wanting to let himself out of her sight, he didn't want to let her out of his.

My mom said to me, "If you're Randa, then you're torturing yourself for nothing over this boy. I don't know whether you'd like him to be your brother, or something else. Do you still think of yourself as the little girl who wants the toy that chose her sister?"

At first I didn't understand what my mom meant by a toy that chooses a person. I did realize, though, that she'd said it from the heart, and that she'd said it in a moment of calm lucidity.

*

Amna was at the hospital with a little boy. A dum-dum bullet had shattered half his spinal column and left him without legs to run with. Gone were the days when he could chase army jeeps, and then come home and tell his mother he'd been playing soccer. The little boy was sobbing, terrified that Amna would rob him of his mother the way the bullet had robbed him of the ability to play, run after soldiers, and make a nuisance of himself at checkpoints.

Suddenly a huge ruckus filled the corridors and the hospital rooms and drowned out the little boy's sobs.

"What's going on?" Amna asked the nurse who was standing at the door.

"There seems to be a wounded child."

"Oh Lord, how long?" Amna said despairingly.

Not long afterward she got up absently like someone walking in her sleep.

Suddenly the cries of the little boy behind her disappeared. She wasn't hearing anything any more.

"What happened?" she asked after the group carrying the wounded boy had passed.

"He's been martyred," one of the young men replied.

"How old was he?"

"Fourteen, fifteen, something like that."

"God be with his mother."

She went back into the room where she'd been staying with the little boy and sat down on the edge of the bed. He wasn't crying. During the less than a minute she'd been away from him, his screaming had stopped. It seemed that the bullet wasn't going to go on robbing him of the good things in his life while he looked on helplessly. It had robbed him of life itself.

Had he really gone silent? His mother had valiantly held back her tears as she pleaded with him to let "Auntie Amna" take him to be with the other children at the rehabilitation center, which, she'd explained, would be "just a school like the one you used to go to."

The voices of the patients, visitors, doctors, and nurses on and around the beds that dotted the large room faded out, and once again Amna found herself rising to her feet. She followed the ruckus, which had turned to a deep silence whose bloody footprints led her down the corridor.

As she made her way with difficulty through the crowd, the space between the emergency room entrance and the stretcher felt like the longest distance she'd had to cover in her entire life. When she got there, she looked into the face of the boy who'd received a bullet to the head. She pondered his blood-drenched features.

"Do you know him?" someone asked her.

She shook her head and left.

She walked back to her house, our house.

She knocked on our door. I came out.

"Where's Nadia?" I asked her.

"I don't know," she replied blankly.

I told her Saleh hadn't come home.

"There's a boy at the hospital who looks just like him."

"How could you tell us apart?"

. . . I ASKED MY MOTHER.

"I don't know," she admitted. "I used to be able to, but I can't any more. And you two are to blame!"

"Actually," she went on, "I don't know if it was you or your sister that mixed me up. You wanted Lamis's name because you thought it was prettier than yours. You'd wail, 'Why didn't you call me Lamis, and her Randa?' We tried to talk Lamis into giving up her name, but she wouldn't do it. We promised her a toy or anything she wanted if she'd agree to trade names with you, but she'd have none of it. 'How will I recognize myself after that?' she wanted to know. 'You'll recognize yourself because you're you,' we told her. 'But,' she objected, 'when somebody calls Lamis, who's supposed to answer? Me, or Randa? And if something happens to me, or if I die, will it be me, or Randa?' She held onto that name of hers for dear life. But I know you two used to trade names, anyway. Don't deny it!"

And I didn't deny it. But one of us went up to the roof that day, and a sniper saw her. All it took was a single bullet, and she was down.

Whenever any of us tried to get to her body, chips of cement would go flying off the edges of the wall that rimmed the roof. The bullets were coming from a distance. We could see them, but we couldn't hear them. It wasn't until two hours later that we managed to traverse the four meters that separated us from her. When we did, her body was lying in a pool of blood, and her name lay there beside her like a little bird. I picked the name up and took it inside as they brought down the body in which the bullet had opened a window of darkness. Then I realized that names were the last thing on people's minds, so I put it away. The weeping and wailing went on and on. Some time later a neighbor saw me crying. Since nobody could tell my sister and me apart, it looked as though I were crying for myself.

The neighbor stared at the body wrapped for burial, and suddenly out came the awful question that turned the whole world into a mass of silence.

"So who died—Lamis, or Randa?"

My mom peered at me through her tears and asked me, "Which of you was it, child?"

I said nothing.

I get up in the middle of the night and slip into the room that opens onto Amna's side yard, the room where we spent time together all those years. I open the notebook, and I read and read until morning, amazed that we lived through all those things.

I walk down the street. A neighbor lady passes me and says, "Good morning, Randa."

"I'm Lamis, Auntie," I reply.

"Oh, pardon me," she says.

A half-hour or so later, I run into her again, and this time she says, "Hello, Lamis. How are you?"

"I'm Randa, Auntie," I correct her.

My mother's started to worry about me. "If you keep that up, girl, you're going to lose your mind," she says ominously.

"But why?" I demand. "Just because I want people to know she hasn't really died?"

"To know who hasn't died?"

And I tell her, "Saleh's the only one who ever knew how to tell us apart. And that's because he was in love. By myself, though, I can't say which one of us it was. So if you want to know which one I am, you'll have to ask him."

One morning an airplane hovered overhead.

It leered down at our street.

A short while later, it dropped a bomb.

We saw it coming, but it seemed to be moving so slowly that we didn't feel the need to run for cover or drop to the ground. Then before we knew it, the blast had sent everything flying. I looked around. I couldn't see anything, even myself. I took off running, and managed to fly through the door that led onto Amna's yard without knowing what I'd done. Suddenly I bumped into a body. It belonged to my mother.

Not long afterward I saw her hands trying to fan the dust away, so I started doing the same. I went on trying to fan it away for hours without it going anywhere.

I heard people screaming and coming from all directions. When everything had quieted down and I got my eyes back, I saw scattered body parts suspended in the air, and nothing was left of the house but two colorless palm trees.

"The tea's ready, Auntie Amna."

. . .

"No, it was no trouble at all! You just take care of Nadia."

. . .

"She knows how to take care of herself, you say?"

. . .

"Well, that makes me feel better."

. . .

"And me?"

. . .

"Like I told you last time."

. . .

"You still don't believe it?"

. . .

"But really: I felt as though the night was all lit up. I went up on the roof, and I wasn't scared. When I looked around, I couldn't believe my eyes. The people in the streets were like fireflies. Granted, they were sad. But still, they were all glowing, and so was I. You know, Auntie Amna, when we can't

make our wishes come true, our sadness gives us the bright-
ness we need. Otherwise, as Grandma says, our light would
have gone out a hundred years ago."

. . .

"You say that's a big dream? No, it's just a dream, that's
all."

. . .

"This morning my mom asked me to write the word
'Palestine.'"

. . .

"Yeah, I did. I wrote it. When she took the piece of paper
in her hands, she ran away with it like a little girl and locked
herself in the other room. When she came out again holding
another piece of paper with the word 'Palestine' written on it,
she was even more confused than she had been before. She
asked me to tell her which one was in Randa's handwriting,
and which one was in Lamis's. Then she started to cry. I told
her, 'Actually, both of them are in my handwriting.' 'And who
are you?' she asked me."

. . .

"You think I should tell her the truth, then, since if I don't
tell her now, then I never will?"

. . .

"Okay, then. I will. I promise."

SELECTED HOOPOE TITLES

Time of White Horses
by Ibrahim Nasrallah, translated by Nancy Roberts

No Knives in the Kitchens of This City
by Khaled Khalifa, translated by Leri Price

The Baghdad Eucharist
by Sinan Antoon, translated by Maia Tabet

*

hoopoe is an imprint for engaged, open-minded readers hungry for outstanding fiction that challenges headlines, re-imagines histories, and celebrates original storytelling. Through elegant paperback and digital editions, **hoopoe** champions bold, contemporary writers from across the Middle East alongside some of the finest, groundbreaking authors of earlier generations.

At hoopoefiction.com, curious and adventurous readers from around the world will find new writing, interviews, and criticism from our authors, translators, and editors.